SPOOKY

Montana

SPOOKY
Montana

Tales of Hauntings, Strange Happenings, and Other Local Lore

RETOLD BY S. E. SCHLOSSER

ILLUSTRATED BY PAUL G. HOFFMAN

Guilford, Connecticut

Guilford, Connecticut

Project editor: Jessica Haberman
Text design: Lisa Reneson, Two Sisters Design
Layout: Joanna Beyer
Map: M.A. Dubé © Morris Book Publishing, LLC

Library of Congress Cataloging-in-Publication data

Schlosser, S. E.
  Spooky Montana : tales of hauntings, strange happenings, and other local
lore / retold by S.E. Schlosser ; illustrated by Paul G. Hoffman.
    p. cm.
  ISBN 978-0-7627-5123-5
  1. Ghosts—Montana. 2. Haunted places—Montana. 3. Tales—Montana.
I. Hoffman, Paul G. II. Title.
  BF1472.U6S323 2009
  398.209786--dc22
                                        2009007037

Printed in the United States of America
10 9 8 7 6 5 4 3 2 1

For my family: David, Dena, Tim, Arlene, Hannah, Emma, Nathan, Ben, Deb, Gabe, Clare, Jack, Chris, Karen, Davey, and Aunt Mil.

And for Mary Norris, Paul Hoffman, Erin Turner, Jess Haberman, and all the wonderful folks at Globe Pequot Press, with my thanks.

For Brian, Art, Renee, and Lennae, with my thanks!

Contents

INTRODUCTION   xiii

PART ONE: GHOST STORIES

1.   *The Watcher*   2
      BIG MOUNTAIN/WHITEFISH

2.   *The Housemaid*   7
      EAST GLACIER

3.   *The Camp Bed*   12
      SWAN LAKE

4.   *Bad Medicine*   17
      MARIAS PASS

5.   *The Merc*   23
      MISSOULA

6.   *The Return*   28
      EMIGRANT

7.   *Quake Lake*   33
      GALLATIN NATIONAL FOREST

8.   *Calamity*   38
      LAUREL

9.   *The Candle*   46
      RED LODGE

10.   *Knock, Knock*   52
      BOZEMAN

11.   *I Want to Go Home*   58
      GREAT FALLS

12.   *The Battlefield*   63
      LITTLE BIGHORN BATTLEFIELD NATIONAL MONUMENT

Contents

13.   *Pray*   70
      HELENA

PART TWO: POWERS OF DARKNESS AND LIGHT

14.   *Foul Spirit*   78
      BROWNING

15.   *The Bleeding Sink*   84
      HELENA

16.   *The Flying Torso*   89
      BUTTE

17.   *The Cowboy's Sweetheart*   97
      CUSTER COUNTY

18.   *The Party*   103
      TETON COUNTY

19.   *Faster!*   110
      VIRGINIA CITY

20.   *Crop Circle*   117
      WIBAUX COUNTY

21.   *Rubberoo*   128
      BILLINGS

22.   *Grizzly*   137
      PARK COUNTY

23.   *Monster*   143
      FLATHEAD LAKE

24.   *Sacred Place*   148
      PRYOR MOUNTAINS

25.   *The Stone*   156
      SHELBY

26.   *Bloody Mary Returns*   163
      BOZEMAN

Contents

27.   *Snow Bird*   172
      GLACIER NATIONAL PARK

RESOURCES   187

ABOUT THE AUTHOR   191

ABOUT THE ILLUSTRATOR   192

SPOOKY SITES . . .

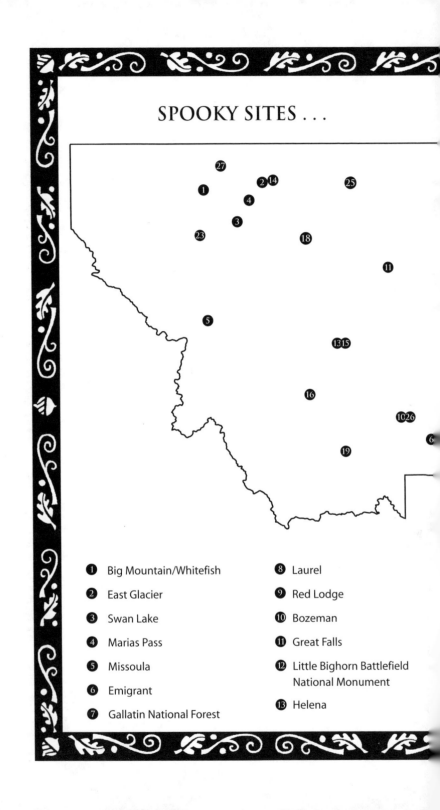

1. Big Mountain/Whitefish
2. East Glacier
3. Swan Lake
4. Marias Pass
5. Missoula
6. Emigrant
7. Gallatin National Forest
8. Laurel
9. Red Lodge
10. Bozeman
11. Great Falls
12. Little Bighorn Battlefield National Monument
13. Helena

AND WHERE TO FIND THEM

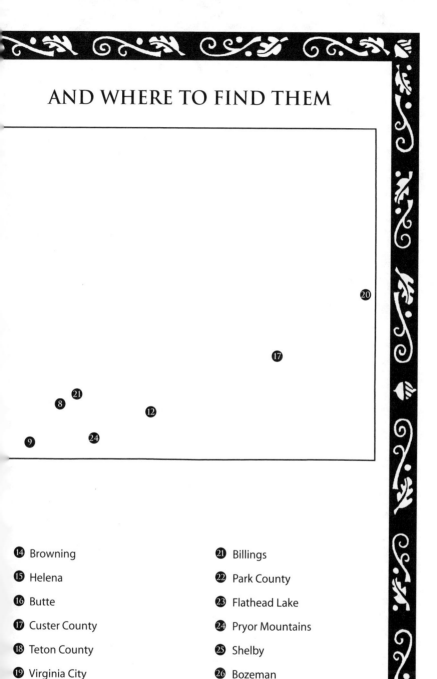

⑭ Browning

⑮ Helena

⑯ Butte

⑰ Custer County

⑱ Teton County

⑲ Virginia City

⑳ Wibaux County

㉑ Billings

㉒ Park County

㉓ Flathead Lake

㉔ Pryor Mountains

㉕ Shelby

㉖ Bozeman

㉗ Glacier National Park

Introduction

I wasn't sure what to expect from my trip to Montana. I was seven years old when I first visited the state, and by now my memories from that vacation were vague. I certainly wasn't expecting the sudden aerial swoop over the mountaintops and the sharp turn the pilot made when we reached Missoula (something my white-lipped seatmate, a long-time Montana resident, said was not the customary landing pattern).

And I certainly didn't expect, as I entered the shuttle that was to take me to my rental car, that I would collect three new ghost stories during the mile-long journey. Or to discover, as I wandered into a downtown department store to follow up on one of the reports, that the entire staff was on a first-name basis with the ghost ("The Merc"). "Oh, you mean Walter," said one of the saleswomen working on the upper floor. Yes, indeed. I meant Walter.

Montana was full of delightful surprises. Everyone told me the scenery there was gorgeous. They lied. Gorgeous is far too mild a term for foggy sunrises cresting over snow-capped peaks; steaming hot springs tucked into the side of looming green mountains; or winding roads that roam past glacier-strewn hanging valleys, with sheer drop-offs that made my heart pound with both excitement and gut-twisting fear. All these things and more were Montana. Gorgeous? Pah! Amazingly beautiful. Heart-wrenchingly lovely. Full of fantastic adventure. Perhaps,

if I spin enough superlatives, I might give you some idea of what Montana is like. But I doubt it. It's something you have to experience to believe.

From Missoula, I wandered past Flathead Lake with its resident monster (be it the ultimate white sturgeon or a true Nessie, I leave it for you to decide), and on to Whitefish, where "The Watcher" stands in the old lodge on Big Mountain, glaring alternately at passing mountain bikers and skiers, depending on the season. From there, I spent several days at Glacier National Park, meeting many wonderful people and happily collecting stories of things that go bump in the night ("The Housemaid"), haunted summer camps ("The Camp Bed"), and dark spirits that need banishing ("Foul Spirit").

One of the defining moments of my trip came when I impulsively stopped at a rock shop in the small town of Bynum and met one of the paleontologists who worked at Egg Mountain, where the Maiasaura dinosaur nests were first found. He guided me through the wonderful collection of fossils in his shop, and I bought many treasures that I cherish still.

From Bynum, I wandered to Great Falls, with its fabulous Lewis and Clark National Historic Trail Interpretive Center and its accident-prone ghost who haunts the road north of town ("I Want to Go Home"). Then I ventured into the state capital of Helena with its impressive historical society, its charming Carroll College campus (which has a spooky story about "The Bleeding Sink"), and its very old folktale—lost for many years—about a dying miner who avenges himself upon the dour wife who made his life a misery. This story instantly became one of my all-time spooky favorites ("Pray").

What else can I tell you of my adventures? I spent several moving hours at the Little Bighorn, climbed up to a pictograph cave in Billings, and wandered underground for several hours in the Lewis and Clark Caverns—a must-see for anyone traveling in Montana! I drove across the Beartooth Mountains in a breathtaking journey that culminated on a snowy mountaintop where, against an amazing backdrop of snowy peaks and misty valleys, someone had constructed a rather lopsided snowman! I meandered my way through Yellowstone National Park, stayed at a haunted ranch just north of Yankee Jim Canyon, swam in the hot springs of Chico, roamed the haunted streets of Virginia City, and panned successfully for sapphires atop a mountain just north of Anaconda. During my wanderings, I collected stories of haunted lakes ("Quake Lake"), strange alien encounters ("Crop Circle"), amazing rescues ("Grizzly"), and murderous revenge ("Rubberoo").

Montana is truly a haunted state! Haunted by beauty, by courage, by good cheer, and, of course, by ghosts. The next time I want to run away from the world, I'm going to Chico Hot Springs. Won't you come with me?

—S. E. Schlosser

PART ONE
Ghost Stories

1

The Watcher

Billy and I took our mountain bikes up to Whitefish Ski Resort on Big Mountain the first day of summer to ride down the Danny On Trail. We'd ridden the mountain bike trail once last summer and found it an amazing ride. We promised ourselves we'd do it often this year since we'd both gotten summer jobs in Whitefish.

We parked and picked up tickets. Then we headed over to the ski lift, chatting eagerly about the anticipated run. There were tons of trails down the mountain, and we meant to explore them all. As we passed underneath the dark chalet that loomed over the ticket office and ski lift, I happened to glance up and see a figure in the third-story window. It was just a dark shape—not fully recognizable from that distance as either a man or a woman—though my gut told me it was male. The person was staring at me intently. It was disconcerting. It—he—saw me looking at him, but his gaze didn't flicker, even for a second. I shivered and looked away.

"Come on, Jerry," Billy called to me. He was already at the lift with his bike. Glad for the excuse to get away from the

2

strange watcher, I hurried over, and we hooked up our bikes onto two separate chairs and soon were sailing up and away over the mountain, on our way to the top. I glanced down at the chalet as I drifted upward and saw the figure in the window, still watching me intently. I shuddered and turned away.

The run down the mountain was just as amazing as I remembered. Billy and I called out to one another and paused occasionally when we spotted a particularly fine view or some wildlife. We reached the bottom in record time and hurried back over to the lift, eager to do it again. I couldn't help myself. I glanced up at the chalet as we passed. It loomed on the bluff over the lift, and the Watcher was still there, still staring at me without blinking. I glared back for a moment, chills running up and down my spine. Then I followed Billy to the base of the lift and helped him secure his bike. This time, I refused to look at the chalet as the lift rose up and above its dark roof. But I could still feel the gaze of the Watcher in the window fixed on me menacingly.

I tried to not let it bother me, but I was so preoccupied wondering about the Watcher and his hateful glare that I failed to heed Billy's call of delight and almost smashed into him when he stopped suddenly to point to a black bear that was ambling away into the bushes on a slope below us. "Watch what you're doing, Jer," Billy called sharply as my bike skidded on the dirt and gravel and I almost fell over. By the time I regained control, the bear was gone. "Sorry," I said to Billy. But I still couldn't put the Watcher out of my mind. I wondered if he would still be standing in the third-story window when we reached the bottom of the mountain. Somehow, I thought he would.

THE WATCHER

And he was. Just a dark figure, not noticeably male or female. Standing in the window, staring at me with malice. Daringly, I waved jauntily to the figure, and Billy looked at me in surprise. "Who are you waving to?" he asked, glancing up at the looming chalet in the bright sun of the summer afternoon. "The man in the window," I replied, gesturing upward. "What man?" Billy asked. The figure was plain to my eyes, but even when I pointed it out, Billy couldn't see it. That really freaked me out.

I was shaking as I loaded my bike onto the lift, and the shaking didn't cease all the way back down the mountain. Billy noticed in the end. "Dude, you don't look too good," he said, as, white-faced, I dismounted from my bike at the bottom of the trail. We were nearly on top of the chalet here, but the figure wasn't visible from the front. Thank God. I only saw him at the back window.

"I don't feel too good," I admitted, something I would never have said under normal circumstances. But having a dark figure invisible to everyone else glaring at you from the top of a haunted chalet was far from normal, in my book. We had to walk right under the chalet one more time to get to the car, and the Watcher glared at me all the way. I could still see him peering from the window as we drove away down the mountain.

At home, I phoned my girlfriend, who had a job up at the resort. I brought the conversation casually to the old chalet, and my girlfriend mentioned that several staff members believed the old building was haunted. When the building became a restaurant, the third floor was closed down to help insulate the lower two floors, and no one—not even security—had a key. Yet people swore up and down that they saw a figure standing in the third-floor window. Creepy. No one knew exactly who the ghost was. Some speculated he was a guest who had died in a ski accident. Others thought he might be a former owner or manager, returned from the grave to visit the old chalet.

Whoever it was, the staff didn't like to visit the chalet after the restaurant closed at night, and I couldn't blame them. I wasn't sure if I would ever go biking on Big Mountain again, despite the gorgeous trails. That strange Watcher had me completely freaked. Next time Billy wanted to go for a ride, we'd go somewhere else!

2

The Housemaid

I've been a security guard for many years at the historic lodge, and I've seen and heard some strange things in my time. I've always had the ability to perceive spirits, a talent passed down to me from one of my Native American ancestors. When I was little, I saw the spirit of my grandfather walk into our house and wander away with my father's jackknife. A week later I saw him return to our house for another visit and put the knife back in my father's bedroom. Other times, spirits have come to ask me to pray for them, and I've done my best to help the poor souls find their way to the light. It's not an easy gift. But it's a gift that has made me comfortable with the supernatural and unafraid of dark powers, which is something to be grateful for. Especially since I work at a haunted hotel.

The main lobby of the lodge is almost four stories tall, ringed with log balconies interrupted every few yards by huge columns made from the trunks of enormous Douglas fir trees—with the bark still attached—which tower over the rectangular lobby below. There is something of the living spirit still in those massive trees, and during the week before the season opened, when I spent the nights alone in the huge lodge, I came to

7

realize that they were absorbing all the memories and energy of the people who came to stay here. At night, I would hear the piano playing and the murmur of voices coming from the lobby, punctuated by faint laughter.

There were also not-so-good vibes coming from the bar below the lobby, but as I said, dark spirits don't bother me. With prayer and a stout heart, you can usually make them go away. If that doesn't help, then a cleansing ritual with a willow switch and a smudge of sweetgrass, sage, and sweet pine does the trick.

The staff at the hotel also sensed the spirits lurking below the surface. I heard them whispering together about invisible voices that spoke out of thin air; about the music box in the gift shop playing music that wasn't recorded on it. Payphones would ring out mysteriously in the middle of the night, and once a couple checked out at two o'clock in the morning, claiming that a phantom woman in high heels had stalked right through their bedroom and disappeared out the far wall. Strange stuff.

Like any hotel that's been in operation for nearly a hundred years, we've had our share of deaths. In recent history, several people have taken bad falls in the road or down the steps. And there was at least one far older and much more tragic death in the hotel, back in the 1930s. It happened in the annex. Apparently, one of the housemaids living on the third floor hung herself, heartbroken over a bad love affair. And since that time, visitors have seen a white figure appear in the windows of the third floor and on one of the balconies. Sometimes, the ghost even appears in the breezeway between the main building and the annex.

Well, the supernatural goings-on finally got so bad at the lodge that the location manager—a practical woman

THE HOUSEMAID

who believed in the spiritual even when she herself did not experience it—decided to have a Blackfoot medicine man come in and cleanse the building once a year. As I said before, the cleansing ritual is powerful stuff. A guest dying of terminal cancer happened to be visiting during the ritual, and he was smudged along with everyone else. And when he got home, the doctors discovered he was completely cured. After the ritual, the building felt better too—for a time. But slowly the murmurs began again, and visitors started seeing a ghostly lady in the third-floor windows of the annex.

Along about this time, I was on night duty, wandering through the spooky hotel buildings long after the guests were asleep. Once, after I checked the doors on the end of the hallway of the third floor annex, I turned and started a casual stroll down the long hallway. And suddenly, I don't quite know how, there was a woman in front of me in an old-fashioned dress that reminded me a little of the clothes of a Mennonite or Amish woman. She was a yard or so ahead of me, and I was a bit puzzled as to how she had gotten there, since I hadn't heard or seen a door opening. Something else puzzled me about the woman, but it took me a few steps to realize what it was. Below me, the old floor creaked and thudded with every footstep I took. But the floor below the woman made no sound. I stared toward her feet, but her long dress obscured them.

By this time, the hair on the back of my neck was standing on end. Something was definitely odd about this lady. She turned when the hallway split, heading for the staircase to the third floor. She passed right over a wooded section of floor that squeaks quite loudly whenever anyone sets foot upon it. But her feet made no sound.

I stood at the bottom of the stairs and watched as she went up one step and then the next. I still couldn't see her feet, and those darned creaky stairs made no sound. It was as if the woman floated up the staircase. And when she reached the top step, she vanished.

I was astonished and ran up the stairs lickety-split. The boards creaked and moaned with every step I took. There was still no one there, but I could feel sadness all around me, and it seemed more concentrated in front of the door of the room where the maid had committed suicide. It was then that I realized that the woman I had seen was a ghost! Probably the ghost of the suicidal housemaid, still wandering the hallways of the lodge where she had died.

After this sighting, things in the lodge seemed to get worse. A family reported a menacing growling sound outside the first-floor window of their room. The ghost woman was seen in the windows of the lodge by several different guests over the next few weeks. One evening, one of the staff workers who'd been with the lodge for many years was downstairs in the bar when his chair was tugged forward by an invisible force and a large cabinet was tipped over on top of him. He was lucky to escape injury.

That was the last straw. The location manager brought the medicine men back in to perform another cleansing and also called in the local Catholic priests to make doubly sure the supernatural activities stopped. And they did. The double blessing seemed to work, because after that, the spiritual activity around the building settled back to a much lower, more tolerable level. Oh, sure, occasionally the sound system doesn't work, and folks can still feel a presence in the basement and on the third floor of the annex. But the dark forces have abated—at least for a time—for which I am grateful.

3

The Camp Bed

SWAN LAKE

It was the sort of story that counselors always told around the campfire to their wide-eyed audience. A haunted cabin, right here in the camp! I'd heard it myself when I was a young Scout sitting next to a flickering fire. According to the story, a counselor had lain down in her cabin to take a nap and had died of an asthma attack before she could reach her inhaler. Ever since, her spirit had haunted the cabin. At this point, the storyteller inevitably added spooky details like icy fingers touching the neck and a glowing form moaning in agony, but I figured those were just details designed to scare the dickens out of little campers.

I had discounted the whole thing as just a good story passed around to all the overnight camps in the area. Until my first day as a counselor, when I stepped into my assigned cabin and knew immediately that the story was true. Don't ask me how I knew. The day was bright and sunny, the lake sparkled and danced before my eyes, and the cabin appeared open and pleasant. It should have been a wonderful moment. But I could see that there were dark shadows in every corner, shadows that shouldn't have been there on such a lovely, bright day. And the

THE CAMP BED

air in the cabin felt heavy and oppressive, as if a presence waited there with malice. I shuddered as I stepped inside.

I was the last to arrive, and there was only one bed left in the room. As soon as I saw it, I didn't want to go near it. It was just a simple camp bed with some shelves and a little bit of room for my trunk, exactly the same as the others in the cabin. But the shadows were thickest in that corner, and the air fairly crackled with the intensity of the dark hatred that oozed out of the walls behind the cot. I was trembling from head to toe as I approached and couldn't help gasping a bit as I dropped my suitcase on the floor by the bed. Oh, lord! I didn't even want to breathe the air beside the bed. How was I going to sleep here at night? Then a few of my fellow counselors bustled in to greet me, and their presence banished some of the dark feeling in the room.

I'd been a camper all my life, and it didn't take long to orient myself to life as a counselor. The kids arrived for their first week of camp, and life grew busy with activities and refereeing outbreaks of war between various campers and doing all the other behind-the-scenes things a counselor does. But every night, I had to return to the haunted cabin and sleep in that dark corner with the lurking, malicious presence. And I hated that. I slept so poorly that I had dark circles under my eyes and tired easily during the day. The camp nurse examined me after a couple of weeks but couldn't find a reason for my insomnia. Somehow, I couldn't seem to tell her I was afraid of my own bed. It sounded ridiculous if you said it aloud.

Of course, the counselors all joked about us living in a haunted cabin, and the story of the ghost with the glowing form and icy fingers was told around the campfire before the first week was over. But none of the others seemed to sense the dark spirit. They treated the whole story as harmless fun.

A few weeks later, I awoke in the middle of the night feeling a cold breeze piercing my sleeping bag. I shuddered and then gasped as something huge and heavy suddenly fell on top of me and began to press me down into the mattress. It covered my whole body. I tried to breathe, but the darkness smothered my nose and mouth, and the weight made it impossible for me to expand my lungs. My body crushed inward under the terrible weight pressing on me. It felt like my ribs were about to snap, and my chest grew red-hot with the need for air.

Above my head, I heard a terrible, heavy gasping and felt hot gusts of foul-smelling breath blow into my poor, smothered face. The whole world around me began to swim as my cold body shook under the weight above me.

One of the other counselors awoke at that moment and shouted in terror. At once, the weight eased and the dark presence faded away. I gave a huge gasp, pulling air desperately into my lungs. Then I fainted, my body slipping out of the bed and onto the hard wooden floor.

I was only out for a minute or two. I awoke to electric lights and a circle of terrified faces. "Oh, my gosh!" one of the counselors cried. "I saw this dark, glowing mass lying on top of you! Are you all right?"

My whole body started trembling, and I waved my hands about feebly, unable to speak for shock. Someone got me a drink of water, and someone else wrapped me in a blanket. After a few sips, I told the group what I had experienced in that benighted camp bed. Everyone was terrified, of course, and we considered waking the camp director, but decided against it. Instead, we pulled my sleeping bag off the bed, and I slept on the floor on the opposite side of the cabin for the rest of the night. And for all the nights that followed.

Once I was out of that camp bed, I was able to sleep just fine, and the dark shadows in the corners of the cabin didn't bother me anymore. I decided, as I packed on the final day, that the camp bed truly must have been the one in which the other counselor had died. I must have experienced her final moments —the pressure on the lungs, the inability to breathe no matter how hard you tried. I shuddered to recall it and decided then and there to get a job at one of the resorts next summer. I'd had enough camp counseling to last a lifetime!

4

Bad Medicine

MARIAS PASS

The railroad man was crazy. Well, all railroad men are crazy, as my father would say. But this particular railroad man was determined to find a myth, and he wanted me to help him.

"How can you find a myth?" I asked him. "A pass through the mountains doesn't exist here!"

He just smiled and asked me to take him to the place where the legend suggested it might be. As I said, he was crazy. But the wages he offered were staggering, and, as usual, I was short on money. So I said yes. Might as well humor him.

My wife didn't like it. Not at all. She scolded me fiercely when I told her where I was going and why. That old story was bad medicine, she said. I nodded. I knew that. But someone had to go along to protect the crazy railroad man. He was a nice, harmless fellow—even if he was a little mad. Reluctantly, she agreed. And she let me go. I was glad. If she had cried or begged, I probably would have stayed home. The woman has me wrapped around her finger, though I wouldn't dream of telling her so. And the idea of pursuing the wild man into such a dangerous place, especially in winter, made me nervous. But I bundled up in my warmest furs, gave my woman a good-bye hug, and set off.

Our journey took us up. And up. And up. The mountains of my homeland were steep and high. Mostly, we wore snowshoes to get us over the deep drifts. Snowshoeing is hard work, and it kept us warm in the frigid air. When we paused to rest and build a fire, the crazy railroad man asked me yet again to tell him the story of the mythical pass through the mountains. I didn't like talking about a place with such bad medicine, but he wore me down. Must be related to my wife.

Many years ago, I told him, too many to count, the tribes living on the far side of the mountains would come through a pass in these mountains to harvest the buffalo. They passed right through *our* land and took *our* buffalo. My people didn't like that. Not one bit. True, there were buffalo for any and all who wanted them. But that wasn't the point. It was our land. Our buffalo. Had they asked us? No. Had they paid tribute to us? No. So we gathered up a great band of warriors and lay in wait for them at the pass the next year. And the tribes came as usual. But with more men than usual—as if someone had warned them we would be there.

The battle we fought then was terrible to behold. Blood flowed like water, and men on each side died terrible deaths, hacked to pieces or beheaded or trampled to death in the fighting. Necks were broken as men fell from high places; hearts were torn out still beating. The few warriors who survived on either side fled for safety at last, for before their very eyes, the spirits of the men lying dead in the pass rose from their devastated flesh to continue the fight. Bad medicine, that was. The worst. The battle between the dead spirits was still waging when our people returned to the pass to claim their dead. That was the last time the western tribes tried to use that pass for their forays into our land. It was full of spirits and bad medicine. And our prowess as warriors frightened away those who did not believe in ghosts. And so the pass was overgrown and eventually lost.

The railroad man didn't speak for a time after I finished my story. Eventually, he picked up a stick, stirred the fire, and said, "I don't believe in ghosts." Then he huddled up in his skins under a snowbank piled high enough to protect us from most of the wind and went to sleep. I told you the man was crazy. Anyone with half an eye could see that the world was inhabited by spirits. I shrugged and added more wood to the fire.

Eventually, we reached the outcropping of rock that my grandfather had shown me, which pointed the way into the pass. As soon as I stepped past it, all the hair on my neck stood on end. Even from here, I could hear the shouts and battle cries and screams of the dying. I stood stock still, and the railroad man looked at me in astonishment. "What's the matter?" he asked. I stared at him, my astonishment even greater than his own. "Can't you hear it?" I asked. "Hear what?" he said gruffly. "Nothing," I said eventually. But he didn't believe me.

I called a halt then, and we built a fire. Then, casually, I waved a hand toward the place where the sounds of battle were strongest. "That way. The pass is that way. Seek it if you must. But I will go no further. When you regain your senses, return to me here, man of the railroad. I will keep the fire going."

The railroad man looked as if he wanted to argue. But something in my face stilled the protest on his tongue. Instead, he nodded. "Very well," he said. Squaring his shoulders, he put his snowshoes on and trudged away, walking toward the terrible sounds of battle that rang through the mountains and made my skin crawl with fear. Crazy man.

He was gone all afternoon. At dusk I threw extra logs on the fire with trembling hands. The battle of the dead still waged on. I could hear it in spite of the cloth I had bound around my ears. And the crazy railroad man was still gone. I wondered if the spirits had found him and ripped him to pieces during their endless fight for the pass. He might be dead himself, for all I knew. But I told him I would wait, and so I stayed where I was, staring into the flames as darkness fell around me. My whole body shuddered with fear, then, and I sat with my arms tightly around my knees, holding my medicine bag in my hands and praying for protection against this evil place and the dark spirits that the night would bring.

With the darkness came the battle, closer and more fierce than before. And now that the brief sun was gone, the spirits were clearly visible around me. Close by—too close—I saw two men fighting hand to hand with bloodstained knives. They rolled past the campfire and disappeared into a snowbank. Their blood made a bright red splash on the white snow, which slowly faded away as I watched. A Peigan horse and rider galloped right through me and off into the trees. A Salish man came plummeting from overhead and landed right on the fire, which crackled and snapped right through his glowing body with its lolling, broken neck before he disappeared. The agonized screams of the dying grew louder and louder. I threw a fur over my head, curled up into a ball, and wept in sheer terror. And then I fainted.

I was awakened the next morning by a touch on my arm. I was stiff and cold. Too cold, I realized in shock. Half-frozen. The fire must have gone out after I fainted. I sat up shakily and saw the face of the railroad man. He was exhausted but alive.

BAD MEDICINE

And I noticed something else, too. The spirits had stopped fighting. There were no longer the sounds of a battle waging in the distance. All was quiet and still and frozen.

"I thought you were dead," I said through chattering teeth.

"No, but you almost were," he said cheerfully, rubbing my hands with snow to bring some circulation back into them. Then he built up the fire again and made both of us a hot drink.

"I didn't even reach the pass until dusk," the railroad man continued. "It was farther away than I reckoned, and the snowdrifts weren't easy to traverse. I figured I'd never make it back without losing my way in the dark, so I broke a hundred-foot path in the snow and walked back and forth all night to keep from freezing to death."

"I can't believe you let the fire go out," he teased me at the conclusion of the tale. I shrugged and didn't explain. If he didn't believe in ghosts, he wouldn't understand.

"My boss will be pleased," he added. "We can bring the railroad through right here."

I said nothing. Normally, I wouldn't approve of a railroad going through our ancient tribal land. But the spirits of the pass were quiet this morning, after the railroad man had spent the night among them. So maybe it was a good thing. Perhaps his railroad would put to rest what our people could not. I shrugged away the thought, stood up, and stretched. "Let's go home," I said to the not-so-crazy railroad man. He grinned and nodded his assent.

5

The Merc

MISSOULA

She was excited to get the job in the new department store that took over the old mercantile building downtown. She liked fragrance and was good with customers. And the money was welcome, too. But for some reason that she could explain to no one, the old building made her nervous. She got goose bumps every time she walked into the store with its bright lights and white walls and too-high ceilings. The store looked brand new, until you noticed the creaky staircases, the molded ceiling in the children's room, and other small indications—behind the updated look-and-feel—that indicated the age of the building. And she hated the cellar. Hated it.

"I feel like someone's watching me the whole time I'm down there," she complained to one of her friends. "It's creepy."

"Maybe it's a ghost!" her friend said with a grin. "Ooh!" Her friend gave a sepulchral groan and waved her hands dramatically.

"Cut it out," the girl said sharply. "I'm not kidding!"

Her friend stopped when she saw how white the girl's face had become at the idea of a ghost in the old Merc building.

The idea would not leave the girl alone. Was the building haunted? Was that why she grew chilly every time she stepped through the door? Why she hated the creepy, dark cellars? The top cellar wasn't too bad, with its bright lights and shelves full of surplus goods. But the cavernous lower cellars that wound underneath the rest of the building, with their dark atmosphere and uncertain lighting, were downright creepy.

Shyly, she approached one of the older ladies at the store one morning and asked her if there was a ghost on the premises. To her surprise, the woman nodded. "That's what the workmen say," the older woman told her quietly. "The building has been renovated a few times over the years, and they say a man in old-fashioned overalls and a plaid shirt sometimes appears in the basement. He'll watch the workers for a moment, then vanish before their eyes. He looks as solid as a real person, but his eyes glow a bit, and no one earthly can vanish without a trace."

The girl stared at her, pop-eyed in wonder, and shivered. "Do they know who it is?" she breathed.

"They think it's Walter McLeod, one of the previous owners of the Merc," the woman said. "One of the workmen saw his picture in a book and recognized him."

"Spooky," the girl said.

"Oh, he's perfectly harmless," the woman said reassuringly. "It's kind of fun to work in a haunted building!"

The girl didn't know whether it was better or worse, knowing that there really was a ghost. She still felt chills when she came into the building, and the feeling that someone was standing behind her watching her every move persisted whenever she went into the cellar. But at least she now had a name for the feeling. Walter.

THE MERC

She wasn't thinking about the ghost the day she went down to fetch something from the lower basement. It was chilly down there, but no more than usual, as she turned and headed down the creepy hallway toward the catwalk leading to the upper basement. A chilly breeze hit her unexpectedly in the face, and suddenly she was staring at a man standing on the catwalk. He looked down at her with eyes that glowed slightly in his friendly face. He was wearing old-fashioned overalls and a plaid shirt.

"W . . . Walter!" the girl gasped, her step faltering.

The ghost met her gaze with a slight smile on his lips. And then he vanished.

The girl blinked her eyes several times, hair standing on end. Her knees were knocking, and she clutched the wall and breathed deeply for several moments before she could move again. She did not want to walk up onto the catwalk. Most emphatically she did not want to walk through the place where she had seen the ghost. But she forced herself up the ramp and heard herself apologizing as she walked through the space where she'd seen the ghost. "Excuse me, Walter," she said as she passed. Was the air a little colder here? A little more solid?

She fled then, her feet carrying her up the stairs and onto the first floor. Skirting the fragrance counter, she hurried over to the woman who had first told her about the ghost and blurted out what she had seen. The woman nodded knowingly. "It's just Walter," she said soothingly. "He's watching over us. That's all."

The girl shivered and then nodded timidly. It was a bit spooky to be sharing space with a ghost. But then she remembered how Walter had smiled at her with the same small smile she sometimes saw on her father's lips when he was pleased with her. She found the thought comforting. Slowly, the shaking in her knees stopped.

She walked back to her counter in a thoughtful mood. She could still feel the presence of the ghost in the building, and it still brought goose bumps to her arms. But she no longer feared him. Walter was just making sure everything was all right in the old Merc. And that was all right with her.

6

The Return

EMIGRANT

It was a tragedy. A fly fishing float trip down the Yellowstone River gone terribly wrong. It happened in June, when the Yellowstone was at its highest and the meltwaters poured down off the surrounding mountains peaks and filled Yankee Jim Canyon with great, sucking whirlpools and dangerous currents.

The young manager of the guest ranch had taken a few young folks out fishing with him, and when the danger became clear, he got them out of the boat quickly, rushing them ashore. But he never made it out himself. The fishing boat was sucked down into the horrible, rushing water and disappeared with the manager inside it. They found the mangled, broken boat a couple of days later, way down the river. It took a full week to locate the body.

It was a tragic time for everyone at the guest ranch. The young husband and wife who worked as assistant managers of the ranch suddenly found themselves running the whole kit and caboodle, problems and all. Probably the hardest moment for the young wife came when she said goodbye to the previous manager's family, who had been excitedly building their new home on the property only a few weeks before the accident. The two wives clung together and cried the day the family moved away.

And then, somehow, the terrible episode was over and behind them. It lingered as a dark cloud in the back of the memory. But time marched on, and there were guests to feed and ranch chores to be done.

One of the chores brought the memory of the previous manager back strongly to the young wife: the completion of the new house where the previous manager had planned to live with his family. It was a beautiful house—a small lodge set into the hillside out of the wind. It looked out over the river valley and had easy access to the horse barn. After much cogitation, it was decided that the house would be set up as another guest lodge and rented out. So the house was completed, and the young man and his wife spent much time there putting the finishing touches on the place.

It was the young wife who noticed something . . . odd about the house. It was a snug home, very well built. But there were strange, chilly drafts that would suddenly sweep down the hall, slamming doors or banging windows shut. She tried to track down the source of the wind, but none was found. The house was too-well built for any stray breezes to blow in. It was a mystery.

The young wife grew uncomfortable working in the house alone. She kept looking up from her painting and scrubbing, feeling as if someone had come into the house, yet no one was ever there. Strain her ears as she might, there were no footsteps, no sounds save her own. But she could not rid herself of the notion that someone was there. A couple of times when this

THE RETURN

happened, a chilly breeze would rise up and slam a door, making her jump and drop the scrub brush.

"You act like the lodge is haunted," her husband kidded her once.

"Maybe it is," she retorted, thinking about the death of the previous manager.

Her husband shook his head a little and kissed her. "Get over it," he told her kindly.

It was hard to put aside the notion. The new lodge was nothing but trouble that first year, as if someone didn't like the fact that the house was being rented out to guests. Slamming doors and windows startled people. Those of a more sensitive nature complained that they felt someone watching them whenever they were inside the lodge. There were unexplained power outages. And once, the basement and first floor flooded.

"You know," her husband said as they were cleaning up after the flood. "You may be right about this place."

Upstairs, a door slammed, as if in agreement.

They kept on renting the place, in spite of the problems. What else could they do? They were running a guest ranch. It was particularly frustrating when the brand-new boiler blew up. However, by this time, they had accepted the fact that the place was haunted, so they quietly had the boiler fixed and kept going.

It wasn't long after the boiler episode that the young wife, on her knees, scrubbing the floor of the bedroom at the top of the stairs, happened to glance over her shoulder and see a man in a brush-hopper shirt and jeans walking down the hall. She gave a start and shook her head a bit, shocked because she'd thought herself alone in the house. When she glanced down the hall again, the man was gone. In that moment, she realized that she'd recognized the figure. It was the previous manager, the one who had drowned before he had a chance to live in his new house. She'd just seen a ghost!

The young wife made a perfunctory search of the upstairs anyway, to prove to herself (and her husband) that there was no one in the house at the time she'd seen the apparition. Sure enough, the house was empty, except for a chilly breeze that slammed a door closed as she left the building. She searched out her husband and found him in an upper field. She told him what she'd seen.

"That sounds like him," her husband said, leaning against the fencepost and wiping sweat off his forehead. "The previous manager was a rodeo cowboy, and I saw him more than once in a brush-hopper shirt. Looks like he's come back to stay."

And so it seemed. They continued to hear doors slamming in the house. And the sound of footsteps in the barn loft was sometimes reported by the ranch staff while they were working in the adjacent horse barn. But after the apparition had shown himself to the young wife, there were no more floods or power outages, and guests no longer complained that they "felt someone staring at them" when they were alone in the lodge. It seemed that the ghost had settled down now that the new managers had acknowledged his presence in their lives.

In the end, the young wife concluded that the previous manager was still looking after the ranch he'd loved, even after death. The thought comforted her, and from that moment on, she no longer feared the new lodge on the hill.

7

Quake Lake

GALLATIN NATIONAL FOREST

It was nice to get away. Of course it was. But I didn't like Quake Lake, and I told my husband so. He just laughed and went his own way, as usual. That's where he wanted to go, and so we went.

I must admit it was a lovely spot. The wind whistled through the trees and riffled the lake into waves. The mountains loomed on the not-too-distant horizon. It should have been peaceful and restful, but to me, it was a haunted place. I shivered as I helped my husband pitch the two-person tent we took on all our jaunts.

Maybe it was the history of the place. The lake itself was created as a result of a massive earthquake that split the land open in 1959, taking a host of park visitors and their cabins, tents, and vehicles down into itself, never to be seen again. The thought of all those people, alive and happy one moment and then suddenly, horribly dead the next, was enough to give anyone the creeps. But it was more than that. The air around the lake sizzled against my skin, as if there were an electric current in it. And sometimes, at the very edge of hearing, there was the sound of voices murmuring. Sometimes, I heard them screaming, which made my ears ring and the hairs on my neck stand on end. And I couldn't bear to look at the ruined cabins on the far side of the lake. Parts of them were still standing, years after the quake. Whenever I glanced that way, they blurred oddly in my sight and made my eyes hurt. Of course Jake, my husband, heard nothing at all, and he laughed at my fancies.

We roasted hot dogs and baked beans over our fire the first night of our trip, then lay back on the edge of the lake and looked up at the stars, identifying each constellation and searching for satellites. Slowly, the strange electric sizzle in the air died away, and my tension died with it. All I could hear were the soft sigh of the wind in the pines, the chirping of crickets, and the gentle lapping of the wavelets in the lake. A sense of peace I had never before felt in this place descended on me as Jake and I cuddled on the lakeshore. We held hands all the way back to the tent and snuggled down contentedly in our sleeping bags for the night.

Some time later, I was shocked awake by a massive jolt that made my stomach roil in fear and pain. I wretched violently, but managed to hold on to my dinner. Frantically, I looked around the tent for Jake—but there was no tent. Just me, my sleeping bag, and the forest. Around me in the darkness, I heard people screaming, children crying. Another of those massive jolts shook the ground and forest, and in front of me the earth split apart and caved in, taking trees and rocks, cabins and tents and people down into its gaping maw, never to rise again. A huge cloud of dust and debris lifted up from the hole, and I could hear the voices of the injured and buried people calling desperately for help from deep inside the rubble in the newly formed crater. Those who had been spared injury were contriving ways to reach them. But the edges of the pit were unstable, and several more sank down into its depths in their rescue attempts.

Gasping, I shook myself out of my sleeping bag, moved by the victims' plight. I had to help! But how? As I stumbled forward in the dust and din and chaos, I saw a mother stagger toward me, holding the hand of her little girl. The mother was bruised and bleeding and obviously in dire need of help. She stumbled a few more steps and fell. I ran toward her, right into a curtain of pure darkness. I stopped abruptly, my body shaking with fear and cold. In the pitch black, the screams of pain and fear and despair grew louder, and even louder. I clapped my hands to my ears, groaning in sympathy. Deep inside, my stomach clenched, and I broke into a sweat as the noise became overwhelming. And then, the darkness was pierced by a small glowing figure. It was the little girl I had seen. She was carrying something that looked like a bag of flour. And then white letters formed against the darkness in the place the ground would be, if I could see the ground. H. E. L. P. The E straggled out a bit, as if the hands that wrote it were shaking. The little girl vanished. Somehow to me, the pitiful message was the worst horror of all. Overwhelmed, I screamed. And then merciful darkness overtook my overwrought senses.

I was shaken awake by my husband. To my astonishment, I was laying once again on the shore of the lake. Jake gave a gasp of relief when my eyes opened, and my big outdoorsy husband actually burst into tears for a moment, hugging me to him fiercely. Staring over his broad shoulder, I saw the dark shapes of the ruined cabins on the far side of the lake. Glowing on the ground beside them were the letters H-E-L-P.

"Jake," I gasped, pointing.

QUAKE LAKE

"I see them," my husband said grimly. "You were right about this place. You were in some kind of trance when you left the tent. I kept shouting to you, but you didn't hear me. Then, when we reached the lakeshore, those letters appeared and you fainted."

Jake shuddered at the recollection and then deliberately turned his back on the cabins.

"Come on back to the tent. We'll leave here first thing tomorrow morning and find another place to camp."

I nodded weakly, and he helped me to my feet. My legs were still shaking as we walked back to our campsite, and I had to work hard to ignore the screaming and crying voices I could still hear echoing across the lake. I was very glad to shut the door of the tent against them, and gladder still when we packed up at dawn and left that haunted place.

I heard later from the friend of a friend that a little girl actually did write the word *help* on the ground in big letters, using a sack of flour her injured mother gave her. But help came too late for the mother, who died of her injuries. The girl lost her entire family in the earthquake that made the lake.

That was our last visit to Quake Lake. After that frightening night, we started going to Glacier National Park for our annual camping trip.

8

Calamity

LAUREL

It was a boring day. Boring, boring, boring. Teddy—he's my younger brother—and I had spent the first week of our summer vacation at our grandmother's farm just outside Laurel, exploring the train tracks and waving to the engineers who drove past at the head of the monster train of railway cars. But Grandmother was frightened that we'd get hurt if we played on the railroad tracks. So now we had to find something else to do.

Grandfather had promised to teach us to ride the ponies that were grazing in the pasture near the house, but the day after we arrived there'd been a bad outbreak of cholera outside town, so he'd been far too busy tending his patients to school us in horsemanship. Being city kids, Teddy and I were a bit nervous about approaching the ponies on our own. So we wandered disconsolately around the yard, wondering what to do.

"We could climb up to the mesa," Teddy said, tossing down the stick he'd been using to rattle the boards of the fence. Teddy's younger than me, and he's usually content to follow me around without volunteering any ideas of his own. When he does speak up, I've learned to pay attention. I looked up. And up. I'd noticed the mesa when we first arrived at Grandmother's house. It looked like it was a couple of miles away from the ranch, and it looked massive, jutting up from the surrounding land with sheer vertical sides. I couldn't see any way to climb up the crazy thing and said so to Teddy.

"There must be," Teddy said. "I heard Grandfather talking to the neighbors about some rotting old cabin at the top that used to belong to someone named Calamity something. They used to keep horses up there. So there must be some way to get up."

I felt inspired by the idea. "Let's go find it!" I cried enthusiastically.

"We can bring a picnic lunch," Teddy said. He was always hungry. Mama said he had a hollow leg, and I believed her. All that food he ate had to go somewhere!

We ran into the farmhouse. Grandmother was busy shaping dough into biscuits, and then tucking the biscuits into a warm corner to rise. She had flour all over her hands and arms, so she smiled as we rushed in but didn't offer us the hugs and kisses that were her normal greeting when we'd been out all morning.

"We've decided to be explorers!" I announced. "We're Lewis and Clark, and we're going to explore the mesa behind the house."

Grandmother frowned for a moment. It looked strange on her round, happy face. "Calamity's mesa," she muttered, pulling out another bowl of risen dough and punching it down hard, as if to relieve her feelings about Calamity—whoever that was. Then she brightened. "Still, that was a long time ago. There's nothing there but ruins now."

Teddy and I looked at each other, staying silent with difficulty. When Grandmother got like this, it was best for her to work things through in her own mind without any prompting from us.

Grandmother looked up from her bread dough. "All right, boys. You just be careful around the ruined cabin. I don't want you cutting yourselves on broken glass or something."

We brightened perceptibly at this tacit permission to go a-journeying.

"We're going to need provisions," Teddy said solemnly. That made Grandmother laugh. She knew Teddy very well.

"There are apples in the root cellar, and you can butter some bread and take that along as well," she said.

Teddy pulled up the trap door and headed into the root cellar while I carefully cut some thick slices of bread and used the last of the churned butter on them. I wrapped up the bread carefully in brown paper with the apples, and we put the packets into our pockets. Then Grandmother gave us directions to the path up the mesa, and we set off.

We walked along the cow path and through a few open meadows, pushing our way through tall, yellowing fields and in and out of a copse of trees. The mesa was ahead of us now. After about twenty minutes of walking, we found the trail up. And up. And up! It was a pretty steep climb, and soon I was panting for breath. We stopped about midway through our climb to eat our snack and stare out at the view of rolling hills and distant mountains. Then we rose and continued.

As we neared the top of the mesa, something strange happened. I walked right through an invisible wall of some kind. It felt like a huge spiderweb that prickled across my skin and made me want to scratch. At the same time I felt a buzzing sensation and heard a high-pitched hissing noise, like a swarm of bees. The prickles and noise were gone as suddenly as they had come, and around me, the sky was suddenly a brighter blue and the air felt crisp and clean and much cooler than it had a moment ago. In front of me, partway up the slope, I saw a figure in buckskins and hat, working on a long fence that hadn't been there before. Behind me, Teddy gasped, and I knew then that he'd followed me through the barrier. I found that reassuring.

Nodding for Teddy to follow, I trudged up the hill toward the gate in the fence. Just then, the fellow in buckskins dropped the fencepost awkwardly onto his finger and started hopping up and down in pain and cussing up a storm. He looked so funny waving his injured finger around that I laughed aloud, making a mental note of some of the more inventive curses he was using. The fellow heard me laugh and turned to Teddy and me.

"You lot got here just in time," he said crisply, shaking his sore finger at us. "Come give me a hand with this fencepost."

When a fellow spoke in that crisp tone of voice, you did what he said. Especially when he had a big rifle sitting right by him. Teddy and I hurried to help.

"You, hold the post like this," he said to me. "And you," he pointed to Teddy, "hand me that wire and those cutters." The fellow in buckskins was all efficiency now that he had a couple of boys to bully. I glanced at him curiously. He had a seamy, dark face and deep-set eyes with a twinkle in their depths. A fairly prominent nose and a mouth that looked ready to smile completed the face, and it was surrounded by shaggy dark hair. It was an ugly face, but an interesting one. And there was something about it that made me look again. The dark eyes rose to meet mine, and I realized suddenly that *he* was a *she*!

41

CALAMITY

"What are you staring at, boy?" the woman in buckskins snapped. "Ain't you never seen a gal before?"

I could tell she was pleased by my reaction to her strange garb and rough ways. "No, ma'am. I mean, yes, ma'am!" I stuttered like an idiot. The woman had that kind of effect on you.

She hammered away at the post, securing it firmly in the posthole she'd dug for it. Teddy packed earth around it, and we both helped her string up the wire. As I moved around the post, I caught a glimpse of a cabin up at the top of the mesa. It looked fairly new to me. Surprising, really, when Grandmother had said it was a ruin. I saw an Appaloosa pony grazing beside it.

"Thank ya, boys," said the woman in buckskin as we rose from our task, brushing dirt off our hands. "That was real kind of you."

At that moment, the buzzing sound returned, and my skin prickled all over. Woman, fence, Appaloosa, and log cabin vanished right before my eyes. I gave a shout of surprise and Teddy gasped. I shook my head, rubbed my eyes. "Where did she go?" I asked my little brother.

He stared at me, eyes round. "I don't know," he replied.

I ran up the slope to the place where I'd seen the log cabin and the horse on top of the mesa. And there was a hollowed-out ruin of a cabin. One of its walls sagging so badly the whole structure tipped to one side. The roof was gone, and bracken grew around and inside it.

Teddy and I stared at one another for a seemingly endless moment. Then we ran. We ran all the long way down the slope of the mesa. I had to run all bent over against a stitch in my side, but I kept going. We paused for a moment when we reached the bottom, and both of us looked back up the long slope. What had we seen? What had we walked into? I looked down at my hands. There was a small scrape on my right thumb where the wire had jammed into it. Teddy's hands were still brown with dust from helping the woman pack dirt around the fencepost.

We staggered home and collapsed in the kitchen chairs. Neither one of us felt like talking about what had happened. Grandmother laughed when she saw us and asked how we liked it up on the mesa. "It's a nice view," she said as she poured us each a glass of lemonade.

"Uh, right. Sure. Nice view," I stuttered, sipping at my lemonade. I'd completely forgotten to look at the view.

"Grandma, who lived in that old cabin?" Teddy asked boldly, wiping away a lemonade mustache from his upper lip.

I looked at him admiringly. I'd wanted to ask the same thing myself, but hadn't been able to work up the nerve.

Grandma's lips tightened a bit. For a moment, she looked totally disapproving. Then she said, rather reluctantly: "It belonged to a woman named Calamity Jane. She lived up there when I was a little girl. She . . . wasn't considered a nice woman. She dressed like a man and acted like a man. She would come to town and get drunk, and sometimes she'd act so wild when she was under the influence that she got thrown in jail. She used to have some horses up there on the mesa. Kept the access path blocked with a fence so they wouldn't roam away."

I remembered the way the strange woman had cussed when she hurt her hand and the way she snapped orders at us. Could that have been Calamity Jane?

"I think I read about Calamity Jane in school," Teddy

said suddenly. "Didn't she ride with Buffalo Bill's Wild West Show?"

"Among other things," Grandmother said. She looked so disapproving that we changed the subject and started asking her when we would be able to ride the ponies.

It wasn't until bedtime that Teddy and I spoke again about the incident on the mesa.

"It was her, wasn't it?" Teddy asked shyly as he shrugged into his nightshirt. "Calamity Jane?"

"It must have been her ghost," I agreed and shivered, frightened by the thought as I had not been frightened by the reality.

"I don't care what Grandma says," Teddy said suddenly, mulishly, as he climbed into the lower bunk. "I liked her. She was nice."

Remembering the sharp, dark eyes with the twinkle, and the ugly but memorable face, I had to agree. I'd liked her too.

"We'll have to read all about her when we get back to school," I said, climbing into the upper bunk and settling myself under the covers. Teddy mumbled his agreement and then leaned over and blew out the lantern. I sighed and snuggled down into the bed. Maybe Grandpa would tell us more about the woman on the mesa when he taught us to ride tomorrow. I smiled at the thought and kept smiling until I fell asleep.

9

The Candle

RED LODGE

Excitement swept through the lodge when Harry and "Jet" (short for Georgette) arrived at the desk to check in. The couple was filthy rich, and Harry, at least, claimed he was looking for a place to get away from it all and indulge his passion for hunting.

Jet was so glamorous that the housemaids gathered on the stairs to gawk at her clothes and sigh with envy. She threw back her black curls and laughed at something her husband Harry said, showing off her long, elegant neck and perfect profile. Then she tucked her expensive furs around her slender form and followed the bellmen upstairs to their suite.

Harry was a bluff type of man whose passion ran to the outdoors and sports of all kinds. The staff of the lodge grew to like him. But Jet was another matter. She might be glamorous, but she was also sulky and petulant and bored. She picked on the housemaids and found fault with everything and anything. Even Harry. Especially Harry, who spent more time fishing or hunting in the hills than entertaining her.

The first night of their stay, the manager gathered the guests around the grand fireplace in the hall and told them

THE CANDLE

stories about the lodge. Including the story about the ghost who haunted the lobby. According to the story, at exactly seven o'clock each night, a lighted candle appeared at one end of the room and floated along its length until it disappeared through the opposite wall. Folks lingering in the lobby at that time sometimes felt a cold breeze and occasionally saw a dim figure dressed in the rough garb of a prospector holding the candle. It was said he died in the mountains while searching for gold. Of course, the floating candle was not visible to just anyone. The people who saw it were either spiritualists—true mediums, not like the famous Fox sisters who pretended to speak to the dead but were later proved to be frauds—or were those destined to die. The manager uttered the last words in a sepulchral tone that sent a shiver through his audience—all except Jet, who looked bored and started to file her fingernails.

Five days after the rich couple arrived at the lodge, a young man named Carlo dropped in to visit them. He was tall and swarthy and handsome. Harry was out fishing when Carlo arrived, but Jet welcomed him with open arms and took him to their suite for drinks. The housemaids shared significant looks when they discussed the matter later that night. Something was going on there, the looks said. Jet didn't mention the young man's visit when Harry return from fishing, and the staff nodded knowingly to one another. But no one said a word to her husband.

That night, as Harry and Jet were sitting next to the fireplace in the lobby, listening to a young man singing very badly and playing guitar, Harry suddenly gave a gasp and dropped his glass of wine. It shattered on the floor, and everyone turned to stare. The guitar player stopped his song midnote, fingers jangling on the strings. Harry's large, hearty face was deathly pale, and his whole body shook. His eyes were following something as it moved from one end of the room to the other. But no one could see anything.

"The candle," Harry gasped, pointing a trembling finger. "Do you see it?"

Everyone strained their eyes, but no one could see anything save the wall and the check-in counter.

"Don't be ridiculous, Harry," Jet snapped impatiently. "There's no such thing as a ghost."

Harry relaxed suddenly. "It's gone," he announced. He was still pale, and his whole body trembled in the firelight. "I think I'll go to bed now," he said abruptly. "Please carry on."

He nodded courteously to the other guests and hurried away, Jet trailing behind him discontentedly as the desk clerk hurried over to clean up the shattered glass and spilled wine he left behind him. Gradually, the other guests resumed their conversations, and the young man went back to playing the guitar and singing badly. No one knew what to make of the incident, and the other guests speculated on its meaning for the rest of the evening.

Late the next afternoon, a hunting party came back to the lodge with terrible news. Harry had been killed when his gun fired accidentally. At least, that's what they thought had happened. Harry had wandered away from the group to answer the call of nature, and a moment later they heard his gun go off and found him lying dead with his rifle beside him. Most of his face was blown away, and the men figured he'd been examining his rifle when it went off.

Jet became hysterical when they gave her the news, and she had to be sedated. As with any unexpected death, the authorities were informed, and they spent several days investigating Harry's death. As the authorities went about their duties, Jet wandered aimlessly through the lodge, dressed in black. She acted as subdued and mournful as any new widow should, but the housemaids said that sometimes, when she thought no one was looking, Jet would smile like a cat licking a bowl of cream. Jet had inherited all of Harry's money, and she was now rich and free to do as she pleased. It was the housemaids' opinion that Jet was not sorry at all that Harry was dead. Quite the contrary. They even wondered if she'd had anything to do with his death, but she'd been on prominent display at the lodge when Harry had his accident with the gun. Then again, there was the handsome Carlo to be accounted for. Who knew where Carlo had been at the time of the accident? But the authorities found no evidence of foul play. A few days after Harry's sudden demise, the authorities decided that his death had been a sad accident.

As soon as Harry's body was released into Jet's custody, she packed up her luggage and arranged for a car to pick her up early the following morning. Then she walked over to the fireplace in the lounge to say her farewells, a beautiful figure in black who played the grieving widow just a little too glibly to be believed.

Jet was sitting in front of the large fireplace in the lobby, graciously accepting condolences and dabbing affectedly at her eyes at every mention of Harry's name, when the grandfather clock on the landing tolled seven. On the last stroke, a cold wind whipped through the lobby. Around the gathered guests, shadows darkened and lengthened, and the fire suddenly went out. Everyone exclaimed in surprise and fear. The overhead lights flickered wildly and then they too darkened.

In the sudden darkness, a candle appeared, floating through the wall to the right of the fireplace. Everyone gasped as it moved slowly toward them, and a tall figure with flaming red eyes and the rough clothes of a gold prospector slowly flickered into being beside the candle. The ghostly wind picked up, and with it came an unearthly howling and shrieking that made the spine tingle and the knees shake. The sound rose higher and higher, hurting the guests' ears and making the hairs on the back of their necks stand on end. The ghost raised a black-nailed hand and silently pointed an accusing finger at Jet, its eyes two pools of fiery red flame.

"It wasn't me," Jet screamed, leaping up from her chair, her wine glass shattering on the floor in a terrible parody of the night before Harry died. "It wasn't me. It was Carlo. I swear, it was Car—"

She gave a sudden, terrible gasp and started coughing and choking. Her hands rose to her throat as if she felt phantom fingers cutting off her windpipe. Then her eyes bulged in the flickering light of the ghostly candle, and she fell to the floor, bleeding from both her eyes and her ears.

In that same instant, ghost and candle vanished, and all the lights snapped back on. For a moment, no one moved. Then the girl at the check-in counter screamed, and the manager raced over to kneel beside Jet. Blood was pouring from every orifice on her face, and she wasn't breathing. The doctor said later that she had died of a massive brain aneurism at the moment she was confronted by the ghost of the prospector.

Carlo fled the country when he heard that his scheme to murder Harry and wed the wealthy widow had been discovered. He was never seen again. Harry's fortune went to a deserving second cousin, who made a large donation to the spiritualist society as soon as all the paperwork was signed, in honor of the ghost that had made him a wealthy man.

10

Knock, Knock

BOZEMAN

I was jolted awake after midnight by a knocking on the front door. I sat up, pulse pounding at the unexpectedness of the noise. *Knock, knock, knock.* The sound reverberated through the whole house. It was a hollow sound that made the hairs rise on the back of my neck. *Knock, knock, knock.*

Beside me, my husband still slept deeply, oblivious to the noise. I rubbed my eyes and stared at the clock. Two o'clock in the morning. Who could be knocking at our door at this hour? The kids were all safely in bed asleep. All our relatives were in good health. I didn't see any blinking red lights outside that might come from an emergency vehicle.

Knock, knock, knock. The sound came again, a rhythmic thumping at the front door. Its hollow noise was almost ghostly and unnatural in its steady beat. There was exactly three counts between each knock.

I did not want to get up. I did not want to answer the knocking. And why should I? That's what my husband was for! I grabbed Bill's shoulder and shook it. "Honey. Honey! Someone's knocking at the door."

Bill didn't stir. I shook him harder. He let out a small snore and turned over in bed. I blinked several times in surprise. Bill was normally a light sleeper. And for that matter, why hadn't I heard a peep out of our daughter Lilly, who woke up at the slightest sound?

Knock, knock, knock. The sound came again, reverberating strangely through the house. We had a small, plain house with no fancy marble or high ceilings. Normally, sounds were muted and didn't carry well. But this knocking sounded like the spirit of doom thudding a door knocker against a dread portal.

Stop it, I told myself fiercely, sitting up and putting on my slippers. Perhaps there's been an emergency with one of the neighbors. It is not—most emphatically *not*—a diabolical spirit seeking entrance to my abode. My mind overruled my shaking legs and forced me across the bedroom floor, out into the hallway, and down the stairs.

Knock, knock, knock. The sound was all around me now, raising the hairs on my arms, sending shivers down my spine. My legs trembled so badly I could barely walk. But I had to answer the door. I felt this instinctively. The knocking would continue until I did. I faced the front door in the flickering hall light. There it was, painted green. Just an ordinary door. But the sight of it made me want to flee. The air was cold, so cold. I shook from head to toe and stood indecisively, staring at the door.

Knock, knock, knock. I could see the door reverberating under the fist of the nocturnal visitor. All my nerves screamed at me to run. *Run!* I ignored them and went shakily forward. I stretched out my hand, grasped the knob—*courage*, I said to my shaking fingers—and wrenched the door open.

To my instant and utter relief, I saw my eighteen-year-old nephew standing in the doorway. He was wearing a threadbare button-down shirt and jeans, and his rake-thin body was framed by wildly falling flakes of snow. His face was pale and his lips were blue.

"Aunt M . . . M . . . Martha," he gasped through chattering teeth. "Please let me in. I'm freezing."

"I shouldn't wonder," I cried, all thoughts of ghostly knocking and dread portals driven from my mind at the sight of him. "Standing there in your shirt sleeves! It's below freezing and you aren't even wearing a coat! What were you thinking to come all this way in the cold?"

I grabbed his ice-cold arm and hauled him into the warmth of the hallway. I shut the door on the snowy night and wrapped my husband's coat around him. Then I led him to the kitchen and put the kettle on to make him tea. "What brings you here in the middle of the night?" I asked briskly, rubbing his freezing hands between my own.

"C . . . cold. So cold," my nephew gasped through blue lips. "I'm freezing, Aunt Martha. Freezing."

The kettle whistled and I rose briskly to pour a hot mug of tea for the boy. Turning, I held it out to him. He reached out to take it—and vanished. I gasped, and the mug dropped from my nerveless fingers. It shattered on the linoleum floor, spilling hot tea all over my bare legs and my bathrobe. I hardly noticed. My own body was suddenly shaking with an intense cold as strong as that felt by my nephew. My nephew who suddenly *wasn't there.*

I ran upstairs and dove into bed beside Bill. It was a dream, I told myself firmly. I must have been sleep-walking. After a few

KNOCK, KNOCK

minutes under the covers, my mind grew drowsy and the whole incident began to feel like a dream. I dozed off.

Knock, knock, knock. I woke with a shout and sat up in heart-thudding terror at the sound. Then I realized it was just the heavy footsteps of my four-year-old as he pounded down the stairs to breakfast. Bill was already gone from the bed, and I could hear Lilly singing in the bathroom.

I sat up shakily, remembering the strange dream I'd had the night before. Or was it a dream? My legs were stinging a bit, as if I had a sunburn. And I was wearing my bathrobe, which I remembered taking off the previous night when Bill and I slipped into bed.

Spooked at the thought, I rushed down the stairs in the wake of my noisy son. My husband was kneeling on the floor of the kitchen, sweeping up the last pieces of the broken mug. He looked up at my entrance.

"Someone broke a mug last night," Bill said. "I don't know why they didn't clean it up. Was it one of the kids?"

I sat down abruptly on a kitchen chair, staring at the mug. "No. It was me," I said in a voice that didn't sound like my own. "I thought it was a dream."

I glanced around for my son, not wanting to frighten him with my story. He was gorging himself on toast and jam and wasn't paying any attention to us. So I told Bill about the knocking at the door, and the sudden appearance and disappearance of my nephew.

I'd barely finished when the phone rang on the wall next to the refrigerator. Bill got up and answered it. A moment later, he handed it to me. My sister was on the phone, and she was crying hysterically. My nephew—her son—had been in a car crash in a remote, mountainous region last night. He'd survived the accident, but had been knocked unconscious when the car had gone off the road, and he had frozen to death in the snowstorm. The medical examiner said he had died around two o'clock, exactly the moment when I first heard the knocking.

11

I Want to Go Home

GREAT FALLS

The wind was in my face and I was flying over the highway on my motorcycle. Flying home at last. It was six years since I had argued with my folks back on the reservation and left for good. I wanted out of the constraints they put on me. I wanted to find my own way. And I had. Well, sort of. Maybe it wasn't the best way. I'd ended up wrangling on a ranch up north. But still, I was on my own, making my own friends without my parents' constant scrutiny. Not a word had passed between myself and the folks since that last argument.

Then one day, I woke up with a terrible hankering to see my mother's face. To hear her scolding me and calling me her Joey-boy. I'm a big man with huge hands and a rough, weather-beaten face after all the time I've spent in the sun. It was funny to see such a tough wrangler's face all teary-eyed with longing for his mother. But so overwhelmed was I by the need to go home that I resigned my job within the hour, and packed my few belongings into a backpack a few minutes later. I'd send for the rest when I got home.

And now I was flying down the roads, up and down over the hilly grasslands, the mountains looming far to the west as the sun set spectacularly in the big Montana sky. I was humming to myself as darkness fell. I would spend the night in Great Falls and then turn east for home. If I was lucky and the weather stayed fair, as it promised to, tomorrow I'd be eating a late supper with my Mama.

I was nearly to Great Falls, the headlight on my motorcycle lighting the road home in front of me, when something big sprang out and across the road. Mule deer, I think. I swerved to miss it and my bike skidded right off the side of the road and went down. I tumbled with it and lay stunned for several minutes, aching all over. My head felt funny, so I eased the helmet off and felt along my dark, longish hair, which was sticky and matted with blood. I wiped my hand clean on the grass and eased the motorcycle off my legs. Yes, I could still move them. One knee was throbbing painfully, but I thought I could stand, so I staggered to my feet, wondering what to do.

I was too dazed to think straight when I saw headlights coming toward me. *Here was someone to help,* I decided fuzzily. I limped onto the highway. There was a screech of brakes, a horrible pain, and my body flew through the air, landing heavily on the windshield of the car. The car shuddered to a halt and I felt myself slide off the car and hit the ground. My head bounced heavily against the pavement, and I heard my neck crack. The whole world went a searing white.

A moment later, I was hovering up and away from the scene, staring down at a familiar figure. His face was framed by dark, longish hair, and he was wearing a familiar rough, plaid shirt and blue jeans. It seemed strange to see myself from that angle. The car doors slammed open and two dazed-looking boys, not more than twenty, rushed into the road.

I WANT TO GO HOME

"You hit him! You hit him," one of the boys slurred as he dropped to his knees beside the still figure lying on the road. (I refused to believe it was me.)

"He ran out in front of me. I couldn't stop," said the other boy, who was only slightly less drunk than his companion.

"I think he's dead," the first boy said, bending down over the twisted figure. "I can't feel him breathing. What are we going to do? They're going to throw us in jail for this!"

"Not if they don't know it happened," the second boy said grimly. "Help me get him up. We'll dump him in the river and folks will think he committed suicide."

I watched in horror as the two boys dragged the limp body to the car and thrust it in the back seat. The first boy scouted around to make sure they'd left nothing behind and found the damaged motorcycle. They wrestled the bike onto the road and managed to get the front end into the trunk of the car. They tied it down as best they could and then drove away in the direction of the river.

I gave a shout of fury and tried to follow. But I couldn't. I was tied to the spot where I'd had the accident. Where I'd . . . I couldn't say it. Couldn't think it. I floated my way to the ground, crawled under a bush, and lay in a stupor for a night, a day, another night. Time flowed strangely now that I was dead. And I was still filled with a terrible longing to see my mother.

I awoke suddenly, my leg throbbing and my hair sticky with blood, convinced that I'd just slid off the road on my bike, in spite of the fact that there was no motorcycle to be seen. I staggered to my feet and saw headlights approaching. *Here was someone to help,* I thought, as I limped onto the highway. There was a screech of brakes, a horrible pain, and my body flew through the air, landing heavily on the windshield of the car. The car shuddered to a halt and I felt myself slide off the hood and hit the ground.

A man came running out of the car and raced right through my body, calling: "Where is he? Where is he?" His wife followed him out of the car, shaking and crying hysterically. They rushed up and down the road, searching.

"I'm here. I'm here," I cried to them as the wife ran right through my body. She didn't hear me. "I'm trying to get home. Can you take me home?" But they didn't respond. They didn't see me at all. Finally, they got back into the car and drove away. I watched their taillights sadly as they disappeared into the distance. Then I went back to the side of the road to drift and sleep until the next car came along.

I don't know how long I slept there. Days, weeks, months. Every once in a while, I'd wake in the night to see headlights coming toward me. And I would be filled with a desperate longing for home. Someone help me. Someone take me home. I'd run out into the road, and the accident would repeat itself. Again. And again. And again.

I don't know how to stop the cycle. I don't know how to get home. I've heard that when you die you go to heaven, but I can't seem to leave this place. I can't even get home to my Mama. So how can I make it to heaven?

Please, won't someone stop and help me? I just want to go home.

12

The Battlefield

The old grandmother sat in the creaky rocking chair on the porch, her dark, wrinkled eyes far away. She rocked to and fro, to and fro, as she remembered a warm June day seventy years ago . . .

She was eight years old and sat next to her mother, playing with a bone needle and a small piece of buckskin, learning to sew a fancy bead pattern on it like the one her mother was sewing on her father's new shirt. Just outside the lodge, her father and uncle sat talking together. Occasionally, her young uncle would look up and make a funny face at her, trying to make her giggle. She was laughing at a particularly gruesome face when the sound of gunfire choked off her mirth in mid-giggle. For a split second, she and her uncle stared at one another in alarm. Then her uncle and her father were both on their feet, grabbing their guns and hurrying toward the sound.

Her father paused for a brief moment to touch her hair and wipe away a tear. "Don't cry, little Flower," he said. "Listen to

THE BATTLEFIELD

your mother." A look of love and understanding passed between her parents. Then he was gone, running with the other warriors toward the sound of battle, and her mother was grabbing a few necessary items and hurrying her toward the far side of the village with the other women and children.

She tried not to cry. Her father wanted her to be brave. But the acrid smell of gunpowder, the loud noises made by many guns firing at once, and the battle cries of the warriors terrified her. And there was blood, too. She saw a woman lying half in and half out of a lodge, and her clothing was stained red. Somehow, she knew the woman was dead, though her mother did not say so.

People were running every which way. Warriors were thundering past them on horseback, heading toward the battle. Old men were shouting instructions over the noise, trying to organize the woman and children. She clung to her mother's hand, and they wove through the panic. Soon, they were out of the village and hurrying through the grasslands toward the mountains. Father would meet them in the mountains, her mother said.

She kept stealing glances behind her as they ran. The shots were coming from several directions now. As the fleeing tribes moved steadily westward away from the battle, she lagged behind her mother and watched warriors chasing U.S. soldiers across the river, along low-slung depressions, and up onto ridges. Farther away, she saw a group of soldiers bunched together on a hill. They seemed to be successfully holding the warriors at bay. Just then, her mother ran back and snatched her hand, scolding her to keep up, so she saw no more.

It seemed to last forever, the horrible, loud noises of battle, the shouts and agonized screams and gunfire. Even as they faded into the distance, the noises still echoed inside her head. Where was father, she wondered. Was he hurt? *Please let him be safe,* she prayed with all her might, tears leaking down her cheeks.

The sounds of battle faded away by nightfall, though it was reported that a troop of U.S. soldiers were under siege on a hillside several miles away. When it was learned the next day that more soldiers were on the way, the tribesmen broke off the fight and the soldiers fled. The girl and her mother searched every face as the warriors slowly rejoined their families, looking for her father. But he did not come.

Almost as soon as the U.S. soldiers had fled, her mother and several of the other women hurried back toward the battlefield to look for husbands and sons who had not returned. She followed quietly, desperate to find her father and her uncle. Maybe they were lying hurt on the battlefield. She would help them. She knew how to tie up a wound. Her mother had taught her how.

The way was long, and she found it hard going with her short little legs. She grew weary, and after a time she could no longer see her mother or any of the other women in front of her. That was when she heard hoofbeats, and someone called her name. She turned, her heart bursting with relief, and gazed up at her uncle. He swung off his horse and hugged her tightly. He smelled of gunpowder and sweat and blood. A rag was tied around one arm, but otherwise he was unhurt. She burst into tears when she saw him and clung close.

"What are you doing out here, little one?" he asked gruffly, wiping away her tears.

"I am looking for father," she said simply. "He needs my help."

Her uncle choked a little, and said: "Let your mother go to him, little Flower. You come back with me."

She shook her head, insisting that she must help her father. Finally, sadly, her uncle whispered to her that her father was beyond help. For a moment, she went still in his arms. Then she struggled against him fiercely. "I want to go. I want to see," she shouted. "I want to see!"

"A battlefield is no place for a child," her uncle said sternly.

"I'll go anyway," she cried almost hysterically. "If you take me back, I'll still go."

Her uncle could tell that she meant it. Reluctantly, he took her up on his horse and rode over the rolling hills to the place where her father had died. There were many dead lying on the ridges and in the depressions near the river. As they approached a tall hill, she saw a place where the U.S. soldiers had sheltered behind dead horses during the fight. Some of the dead soldiers were draped over the horses' bodies, and some were lying just behind them. Her father's body lay on the far side of the hill, near the buckskin-clad figure of a blond-haired man. Her mother was kneeling beside her father, unmoving, holding one of his hands pressed against her face.

The girl slipped off the horse and ran to her mother's side. For a moment, she stared at her father's beloved face; his eyes fixed open in death. Then, with a cry of fury, she ran to the nearest uniformed figure and kicked and kicked at it, wailing out her pain. Her uncle leapt off his horse and ran to her, pulling her into his arms, away from the dead soldier. "We made him pay, little Flower. We made them all pay," he said.

Hearing her daughter's cries, her mother roused at last from her shocked stupor. She came to hug them both, and they cried together. Further down the slope, she could see other women searching the coulee, looking for their loved ones, their faces set with the same grief that welled in her heart. In other places, warriors were stripping the dead soldiers of the guns and clothing they no longer needed.

Why, she wondered, staring out over the battlefield with its dead, her heart heavy with grief. *Why had this happened? Why did her father have to die?* It was a strangely adult thought. Perhaps the very first one she'd ever had. For a moment, her eyes lingered on the face of the blond man in buckskins. He had a fancy mustache on his white-skinned face, she noticed. He looked proud, even in death. She turned away from the man and helped her mother and uncle retrieve the body of her father and carry it away.

The soft creaking of the rocking chair was the only sound on the porch until her great-grandson pulled into the driveway with a wave and a short honk on the horn. A few moments later, he gently helped her into the car, and they drove silently together through the long, rolling hills. This was a time for reflection, not speech.

It was dusk when they reached the hillside. They left the car together, and she wobbled up the hill on knees that had grown shakier with each passing year. When they reached the place just below the monument where her father's body had lain in death, she knelt with the help of her great-grandson and placed tobacco on the spot. Then she looked up across the battlefield. Seventy years ago to this day, her father had bravely fought General Custer's men, trying to protect his family and his way of life, and had lost his life during the fight. Her people had won the battle that day, but they lost the war and ended up on a reservation.

As she gazed across the valley toward the river, she saw blue lights appearing one by one and moving gently across the ridges and valleys of the battlefield. The closest light slowly became the shimmering shape of a Lakota woman, searching among the dead for her husband. Another blue light appeared, hovering beside her great-grandson, who was kneeling in the same place her mother had once knelt.

"Don't cry, little Flower." She distinctly heard the words in her mind, and the voice was that of her father. She closed her eyes, and for a moment, the pain of parting was as fresh as it had been that horrible day seventy years ago. Then it faded, and she took her great-grandson's arm and let him help her to her feet.

"Goodbye, father," she whispered. Then they left the battlefield to its ghosts, and went home.

13

Pray

HELENA

He was a jolly, round little man with a cherry-red face and a button for a nose. His mouth was all smiles, and he loved to make puns and tell funny jokes to every person who passed by. He sat every day in the front window of his house with a bottle of whiskey at his side. He would beckon folks over to the windowsill, put up the pane of glass, and tell them his latest riddle or story.

Folks in town shook their heads over little Simeon, but they liked him. He would tell the children strange and wonderful stories about faraway places and magical beings. Everyone wondered how he knew such tales, for they never saw him reading or writing or doing anything except sitting in his chair. He never did a lick of work, as a matter of fact. Folks in town said he'd ruined his health in the mines long ago, and his heart was too weak for him to do anything but sit around and watch the world go by.

Simeon's wife, on the other hand, was tall and spare and dour. She wore gray on weekdays and black on Sundays, and a large crucifix hung around her neck. And she was as hard-working and critical as Simeon was lazy and kind. She despised

PRAY

her husband's indolence. Every day, before she left to clean at the mansion house in the city, she would stop in front of her husband's chair, glare at her rosy-cheeked spouse, and say sternly: "Pray, Simeon. Pray for your soul. If you cannot work, then pray!"

Simeon beamed at her and said: "Yes, Constance." But no one ever saw him pray. Not once. Nor would he go to church on Sunday or on high holidays. Even on the coldest day of winter, Constance would bundle herself up against the fierce winter winds and march stolidly downtown to church, where she would pray for hours on her hands and knees before marching home again. But jolly, round Simeon just sat in the window and smiled as the world passed by.

"Pray, Simeon," Constance would thunder at him as she marched to and from the church. "Pray!" But Simeon refused to pray.

Simeon told the local minister once that he'd lost his faith down in the mine, when the shaft had caved in on him and he'd lain for hours in the darkness, hallucinating as the air grew more and more poisoned. "God abandoned me down there," said Simeon. "I prayed all day and all night for him to send an angel to rescue me, and the angel never came. If my shaft supervisor hadn't come a-looking for me, I'd have been dead. And he didn't get there in time to save me heart and me lungs. They were wounded s'bad I couldn't ever work again. After that, I cursed God and the angels. They'd abandoned me, so I abandoned them."

It seemed wrong somehow, to see such a happy, jolly fellow so solemn and stern. The local minister didn't know quite what to say. He wanted to point out that the shaft supervisor might be considered, by some, to be an angel sent by God. But something in little round Simeon's eyes defeated this idea before he could form it into words. It would have been easier to defend his faith if Simeon had been passionately angry or bitter. But such matter-of-fact heresy was impossible for the minister to combat. So he didn't try. He just told Simeon he would pray for him.

When he heard that familiar word, Simeon's jolly face twisted as if he'd bitten into a lemon. For a moment, he looked strangely like his cross and dour wife. "Pray!" he spat out the word. "That's what Constance says. She says my disability was caused by my lack of faith. Me, who went to church faithful every Sunday since I was a lad! Don't pray for me, minister. I'm done praying!"

The local minister went away, shaking a little at the depth of bitterness in jolly, round Simeon. Who could ever guess such darkness lay at the heart of the happy relater of riddles and jokes, the wonderful storyteller whom all the schoolchildren adored?

And always, looming in the background, grimly cleaning the house and scolding him night and day, was dour, gray Constance. "Pray, Simeon! Pray, you sinner," she'd cry out so loud that the neighbors on both sides could hear her. "Get on your knees, and pray!" But Simeon never prayed. He never did anything but sit in the window and watch the world go by.

Never once did anyone hear him raise his voice to Constance, though she made his life a misery with her scolding and her dire predictions. He rose above it, smiling at her and nodding in agreement with every scornful sentiment. But he rarely left his chair, and he never went to church, and he drank deeply of the whiskey in the bottle, for—had she but known it—the drink helped to mask the pain that grew worse day by day.

73

Simeon was telling his latest riddle to a group of businessmen on their way home from work one evening when he gave a sudden gasp, right before the punch line. The whiskey bottle slipped from his grasp and smashed on the floor. And little round Simeon dropped dead, just like that, slumping forward until his forehead lay across the open windowsill.

They shouted for Constance, and one man ran for the doctor, but they all knew it was too late. Simeon had gone to meet his Maker, happy of nature and bitter of soul. All Constance could say, when she saw him lying in the window was: "Pray, all of you. Pray that this doesn't happen to you. Pray!"

The men backed away from the little round body of Simeon, unnerved by the grim, gray presence towering behind him like a vengeful spirit. Constance's eyes were sparkling with manic fervor, and the men were grateful to turn her and poor, dead Simeon over to the doctor and walk away.

Everyone in town was stunned by Simeon's death. They'd heard that he was poorly, but he'd never shown it. Only the doctor had known the true state of things. Had known that Simeon's poor, injured heart was slowly losing ground. Had put strong medication in his whiskey to help him with the pain. Not even his dour and grim wife had realized that Simeon's laziness stemmed from true illness. Not until it was too late.

The children, especially, were devastated at his death. They'd come every day to the window to listen to his stories, to hear his jokes. He was "Uncle Simeon" to every boy and girl in town. And they were heartbroken to lose him.

Everyone in town came to the church when the huge bell tolled on the day of the funeral. There wasn't a dry eye in the place when the minister gave the eulogy, standing beside the closed casket. Then he asked Constance to speak. Constance stood up beside her seat, black veil quivering with her intensity, and spoke only one word: "Pray!"

The word echoed and reechoed around the great hall. It seemed to grow louder with each echo. One by one, the candles around the altar blew out, until there was only a shadowy darkness behind the casket. Outside, the sunlight was dimmed by dark storm clouds until the interior of the church took on a ghastly, greenish tinge and quivered with the electric intensity of an approaching storm.

And a voice from nowhere repeated Constance's message from the air above the altar. "Pray," it whispered. "Pray!" And then it thundered the word: "Pray!"

A ball of light appeared above the minister's head and grew larger and larger until it formed into the round figure of Simeon. His red face was twisted with pain and anger, and his eyes were fixed on the black-veiled figure of Constance.

"You gave guilt when you should have given compassion," he cried, his round body slowly elongating and twisting into a huge, foul parody of a man. The shadows in the hall darkened, and the children whimpered in fear and clutched at their frozen parents. Simeon's ghost shone with an eerie light that made every face in the watching congregation appear grim and hollow-cheeked. Towering taller and taller above the altar, his round form began pulsing from dark gray to blinding white in a way that stung the eyes and made people's skin crawl.

"You gave scorn instead of understanding," he boomed, raising one arm slowly and pointing a finger at his wife. "And hatred instead of love." The light within Simeon's massive form wriggled and writhed as if a thousand maggots were eating his spirit flesh.

Constance gasped and shrank back from the terrible, pulsating figure. Every eye in the church was fixed upon him in horror as he leaned closer and still closer to his wife, his massive face pressing into hers.

"Pray, Constance," Simeon said, and his voice was suddenly happy and gentle. "Pray for your soul." Then his twisted figure shot suddenly upward until it reached the arched ceiling far above. *"Pray!"* Simeon howled, his voice rising until stained-glass windows started shattering. Everyone in the congregation bolted out of the doors and windows into the biting wind and thunderous rain, their hands clapped over their ears. A bolt of lightning lashed forth from the heavens and crashed into the large oak tree in the center of the graveyard adjoining the church. And then Simeon's wailing voice ceased as suddenly as it had started. The congregation stared at one another in consternation, wondering what was going on inside the sanctuary. For a moment, they stood still as the rain pelted down upon them. Then, one by one, dreading what they would see, they crept back into the sanctuary.

Inside, the candles had flickered back into life, and the air was once more warm and sweet with incense, the atmosphere gentle and sorrowful and kind. And slumped on her knees in front of the altar beside the closed casket, her hands clasped in an attitude of prayer, was the stiff and still figure of Constance. Her forehead touched the floor, and her wide-open eyes were fixed in an expression of fear and dread. Blood trickled slowly from both her ears. She was dead.

PART TWO
Powers of Darkness and Light

14

Foul Spirit

BROWNING

I knew there was something wrong as soon as I put the key in the lock. I could feel some kind of foul spirit emanating through the door even before I turned the handle. Gah! This was too much. Too much! Hard enough to attend a welcome-home-from-prison party for my no-good uncle. Now this!

I slid the door open cautiously and turned on the light. The sense of wrongness was fading now, and I wondered if I had imagined it. Maybe it was just the bad feelings I had during that farce of a party. I heard a happy thrumming, and my cat came to rub against my legs, purring with delight. Around me, the soft, familiar smell of the herbs I had drying in the kitchen mixed with the faint floral scent of the cleaner I'd used to scrub the floor of the bathroom. It was the smell of home. My nostrils twitched a bit, and I relaxed.

As I put down my things and shrugged out of my jacket, I saw the sailboat painting on the wall, the red pillow on the sofa, a half-read book lying on the table. Reassuring things. A puff of breeze blew through the room, and with it came a soft voice: "Help me!" For a moment I froze, but I was too experienced in the spiritual arts to be frightened for long. I knew that voice. It was one of the many spirits who sought my assistance to bring peace to their eternal souls. There were always a few around. If I listened carefully, I could hear the murmur of their voices at the back of the beyond. I relaxed further, took a deep, meditating breath, and listened. Listened. It took a lot longer than I expected for me to connect with the spirit realm this evening. The voices were there, but they were fainter, as if some foul spirit had frightened them away.

I made myself a pot of tea in the kitchen and then sat at the table with the cat in my lap, senses outstretched for the leeching acid feeling I'd sensed when I opened my door. I felt nothing. Too much nothing. It made me uneasy. I should be sensing more than this in my apartment if it were a usual day. My own vibrations, or the soft murmur of a spirit needing words of wisdom or consolation. Or just a happy background hum of a life at peace with itself. But the air was empty and still. It made my flesh crawl, that emptiness. I kept seeing the face of my uncle as his family and friends toasted his new freedom. Why I should see his face puzzled me, but I knew better than to ignore my instincts.

"Enough of this!" I announced to the cat. "Time for bed."

I washed up and crawled under the covers of my bed, tired out from the day's work, the late-evening party. As I dozed, my cat came into the room, purring, and settled on my feet, as usual. Comforted by the feeling, I fell asleep with my hand tucked against my cheek.

A few minutes—or was it an hour—later, I felt my cat walking up the bed toward my face. Strange. My cat usually spent the whole night on my feet. I smelled the cat's meaty breath in my face, felt the tickle of whiskers. My instinct was to reach out and pet him. But suddenly, claws raked down my hand, and the cat bit me, hard. I gave a yell of pain, thrashing out at the cat with my arm. I hit something soft and heavy, and it fell to the floor. I heard footsteps scamper under the bed. Then silence. At that moment, I became aware of a heaviness on my feet. I looked blurrily down the length of the bed and saw the cat lying on my feet, fast asleep.

The sight of the cat made my pulse throb in fear. I'd just tossed the cat off the bed. Hadn't I? Yet here it was, unmoving, on my feet. I swallowed against a suddenly dry throat. If the cat was on the bed, then what had just scampered under it?

Don't be ridiculous, I told myself firmly. You just had a bad dream. Ignoring the evidence of my throbbing hand, I rolled over onto my stomach and punched the pillow into a more comfortable position. At my feet, I felt the cat shifting position with me without waking up.

I had started to doze when once more I felt the soft thud of footsteps walking on my body. The cat was moving again. Yet it couldn't be, since the heavy feeling against my feet was still there. Suddenly, claws ripped across my back, tearing my nightshirt, and something bit me. I reached back, grabbed whatever it was by its hairy body, and threw it with all my strength against the closet doors. It hit them with a loud bang and then thudded down to the floor. I heard something make a mewling sort of grunt, and then footsteps padded out the bedroom door and into the living room. At my feet, the cat stirred as footsteps began pacing back and forth, back and forth across the living room floor. The cat lifted its head to listen and growled a little from its place at my feet.

FOUL SPIRIT

"Get out and stay out," I said firmly to the creature in the living room. The footsteps paused then resumed their pacing. Back and hand stinging, I lay awake listening until the footsteps stopped. Then I fell into an uneasy sleep.

The next morning, I found a huge scratch on my hand and another on my back. There were no signs of the two bites I'd received, but the scratches were very real. Of the foul creature who had administered them, there was no sign. It had been far too big to be a mouse or a rat or some other animal that might creep in through a crack in the wall or floorboard. And there was no open window or door that might admit a larger creature. Besides, I knew as soon as I touched it the second time that it was a nasty, foul, spirit-creature. An all-too-real spirit, if it could cut people with its claws.

At the urging of my family, I phoned a local medicine man and told him my story. He came at once to cleanse the apartment, chilled by the story of an apparition that could cause physical damage to a person living in this world. He spent a long time over the ceremony and smudged me with an herbal mixture as part of it. As soon as I was smudged, a heavy burden that I had not even realized I was carrying suddenly eased, and I felt lighter. The medicine man told me that the foul spirit in my apartment had been riding someone called Jim before it came to me. He asked me if I knew a Jim, and my pulse throbbed at the name. "My uncle, who just came home from prison," I told him. The medicine man nodded gravely. "That is your source."

When he finished his work, the apartment felt clean and airy again, and I could hear the murmur of spirit voices faint in the background, as I should. The foul spirit was gone.

"Thank you," I said gratefully. He just smiled at me, and asked me about the murmuring voices. We spoke then at length about our differing spiritualist abilities, and he gave me some good advice about what to do when the spirits came to me for help. Then he was gone, and I was alone in my apartment again. My cat came and rubbed up against my legs. For a moment I flinched. Then I chuckled, picked it up, and went to make a pot of tea.

15

The Bleeding Sink

HELENA

I found it extremely annoying that one of the bathrooms on my dorm was permanently closed. Especially since the cause was an urban legend. An urban legend, I tell you! According to the story, years and years ago some bloke got himself massively drunk at a bar in downtown Helena and had passed out in the bathroom on the fourth floor. Apparently, he hit his head on the sink as he fell, and his blood had spattered the sink as he slid senseless to the floor and silently hemorrhaged to death. His death was considered a "sad accident" by faculty, staff, and townspeople. But that was no reason to shut up the bathroom for decades! I completely discounted the story of the bleeding sink. That was just an urban legend the students circulated to explain the locked door.

"I'm sick of sharing a bathroom with you disgusting lot," I grumbled to my roommate. "I'm going to break into the fourth-floor bathroom."

My roommate's eyes widened. "Don't you know that bathroom is haunted?" he exclaimed. "They say the sink still has fresh bloodstains on it that won't go away, no matter how hard you scrub. And sometimes," he lowered his voice to a dramatic whisper, "sometimes, you can still hear the boy moaning."

"Romantic twaddle," I snapped. "My granny lives in a haunted castle in Scotland with ghost stories that would make your hair stand on end. She'd laugh at me if she found out I ignored a perfectly good bathroom because of a few bloodstains. Besides, the maintenance staff told me the bathroom was shut up pending renovations. No big deal!"

"You'll be sorry," my roommate said darkly. I ignored him. He was just sore because I'd lumped him in with the disgusting lot of fellows who mucked up the bathroom on my floor. You'd think someone would teach them to pick up their dirty clothes and clean the sink once in awhile.

When the dorm quieted down for the night—which wasn't until late—I hurried up to the fourth floor with a bit of wire I'd purchased at a local hardware store. My little brother and I had become expert lock-pickers over the years, since our mother had a bad habit of locking her keys in the house or the car at least once a week. With all that experience, the lock on the bathroom door gave me no problems.

The bathroom was rather old-fashioned and had a disused air. There was dust in the corners, and a spider web drooped from the ceiling. But I heard no unearthly groaning, no mysterious footsteps. I carefully inspected the sink, the walls, and the floor. Other than a smallish orange discoloration on the sink, there was no blood anywhere. Ha! So much for urban legends. There was probably something in the water that caused discoloration over time. I turned a tap experimentally, sure that the maintenance staff had shut off the water long ago. To my surprise, water gushed forth instantly. I smiled. Well, well. It looked like I had a bathroom to myself after all! I carefully locked the door behind me when I left.

I got up late the next morning and had the downstairs bathroom all to myself. So it wasn't until evening, when everyone was back in the dorm, crowding in and out of the bathrooms, that I slipped away to use the locked-up facilities. It was still early in the evening, and I made sure no one was around before I headed to the abandoned bathroom. With a few twists of the wire, I opened the lock. As I stepped inside, the air temperature plummeted twenty degrees or more, and my nose was hit by the pungent, strong smell of fresh blood. A second later, I saw the blood-spattered sink. Bright-red gore was everywhere—on the porcelain, on the walls, oozing down the sides of the sink. And hovering before it, his feet a good six inches off the ground, was the luminous form of a college-age boy wearing old-fashioned clothes in the style of the 1960s. His forehead had a disfiguring dent smashed into it, and blood was dripping down his face. As I gaped at him, horrified and frozen in terror, he turned and looked at me. Then he held out a blood-stained hand. His eyes were desperate, pleading for help, and I heard a low moaning sound coming from between his blood-stained lips. The sound raised every hair on my body and made my skin prickle in sheer, cold horror.

I hurried backward, my legs scrambling to get away while my eyes and head remained fixed on the ghost, on the bloody sink. A drop of red blood fell from his outstretched hand as I stared at him. Finally, my legs carried me out the door, which slammed shut after me, and the hot, pungent smell of fresh blood followed me through the halls and down the staircases until I was outside in the chilly air of autumn, breathing deeply. My knees shook so badly that I fell onto the nearest patch

THE BLEEDING SINK

of grass, stomach heaving. Oh, lord! The ghost was real! No wonder they kept the place locked up.

I lay on the grass for a long time, ignoring the chill in the air. This was a natural chill that comforted, not that unnatural chill that had frightened me upstairs. I breathed in and out, in and out, watching the stars above me, bright even through the campus lights. I took comfort from the huge, clear expanse of sky. Big sky, they called this state, and the sight of it calmed me. That sky had been here long before the ghost, and would remain long after every building here had turned to dust.

I had no one else to blame for my fright. They'd warned me about the ghost. But I still felt reluctant to go back inside that haunted building. I shuddered once, from head to toe. Oh, how my granny would laugh if she knew her big, brave grandson was too scared to go back inside a haunted dormitory. It was the thought of granny that got me back onto my feet and upstairs to my room. But I didn't care what granny or anyone else thought of me. I was never going back to the fourth-floor bathroom. Once was enough.

16

The Flying Torso

BUTTE

It was one of those beautiful days in September when the snow is just dusting the tops of the mountains and the air is crisp and clear. There were three of us waiting for the lift—me, the shift manager, and a young fellow who was going to be my new partner. The shift manager wanted to check out the site of a cave-in that had happened the previous night to make sure the mess had been cleaned up properly. The shift manager was a tad nervous about the cave-in, and he rattled on and on about it as the lift rumbled up to us. I didn't like such talk. It was bad luck to talk about a cave-in, and I wished with all my might that he would shut up about it.

The small lift seemed unusually spacious as we three got in. Usually, it was packed with six to eight miners, and we had to carry our lunches on our heads on account of there not being enough room for us to carry them in our arms. But today I kept my lunch box tucked into my elbow and frowned mightily at the shift manager as the lift grumbled and rumbled and banged its way down and down into the pitch darkness, lit only by the lights we wore on our helmets.

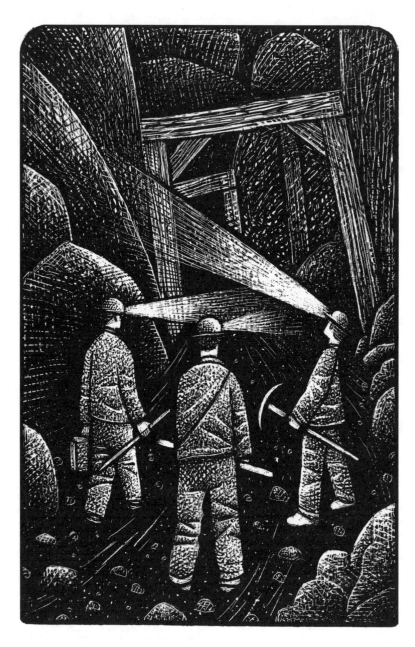

THE FLYING TORSO

"Funny thing happened last night just before the cave-in," the shift manager shouted above the whine of the elevator. "The lift bell rang at twelve hundred feet!"

I frowned at the dark, swiftly passing walls outside the lift. At the moment, there was no one working down at twelve hundred feet. How in the world had the bell gone off? I shivered as the shift manager continued: "We didn't know what to make of it, so we sent down the lift. But it came back empty. So we sent one of the managers down to check it out—see if anyone'd gotten trapped down there or something. The manager came back up that lift a sight faster than he went down. Said there weren't nobody down there, but his face was white and his knees were shaking so bad he could hardly stand. He'd seen something down there, all right, but he wasn't talking. An hour later, the roof caved in at four hundred feet. Strange doings."

The shift manager concluded his tale as the lift stopped off at four hundred feet—the shaft with the cave-in. We stepped off the lift into pitch darkness. The bulbs lining the tunnel had all burnt out. I swore, and the staff manger gave a yelp of anger. "Jehoshaphat, will you look at that! Someone should have reported this."

The youngster gave a shudder of fear, but composed himself enough to gasp: "You . . . you think it's a short somewhere?"

"Of course it's a short!" the shift manager snapped. "Come on, let's take a look at the cave-in site."

Now, I'm not afraid of the dark. Some fellows hear footsteps and soft giggling voices and other things that aren't there when the tunnels get too dark. But not me. I didn't believe in spirits or Tommy Knockers or any other creatures. Hokum! That's what it was. I strode right out into the dark tunnel after the shift manager without a qualm, even though the only light came from the three small beams shining from the tops of our helmets.

The youngster hung back for a moment by the lifts, but being alone down there frightened him worse than being with us, so he swiftly caught up and stalked along at our heels as we threaded our way through the stony tunnels and beams and equipment. And suddenly, the tunnel ended in a huge pile of broken beams and rubble. The cave-in. I cursed and the shift manager swore so much the young fellow turned bright red with embarrassment.

"They didn't even try to clean up this mess," the manager said in disgust. "I'm going to have to report this right away. The youngster can come with me and find an electrician to fix the lights. You okay staying down here and starting the clean-up?"

He addressed the question to me and I shrugged my agreement. The manager left me the battery lamp and walked back to the lift with the youngster while I picked up a shovel and started cleaning. It was back-breaking work, and the tunnel was pitch-black at the edges where the light of the battery lantern and my headlamp did not reach. It was a queer sort of darkness that seemed to leech the light away, and it seemed to suck at my mind and make my hands shake. The noise of the lift faded swiftly away, leaving me all alone in the mine shaft. Alone at four hundred feet. The thought made me uncomfortable.

As I said before, I don't mind the dark, normally. But somehow, I didn't like this darkness. It reminded me of the old tales my granny told of men who turned to wolves and stalked their prey through the old forests of Europe; of vampires who sucked the blood of men and flew through the air like bats; of demons and foul spirits and monsters. My flesh was creeping under my rough work shirt, and the sweat on my hands was the cold sweat of fear, not the hot sweat of my labor. "Stop it!" I scolded myself aloud, pushing my shovel fiercely into the debris. In my mind, I thought I heard the ringing of the lift bell down at twelve hundred feet, where no human worked. It echoed and reechoed in my ears, and my body started trembling. This was nonsense! There was no such thing as ghosts!

At that moment, the light of my headlamp began to flicker wildly. Off, on, off, on. It strobed in a way that made my eyes ache. And it wasn't the only strobing light in the tunnel. The battery lantern was flickering too—in the exact same rhythm as the headlamp! That just wasn't possible. The batteries of both lights were brand new, and they certainly were not wired on the same circuit. Yet each light flickered off and on at exactly the same moment, against all the laws of probability. The sight made me go cold all over. The flickering light was so disorienting that I almost dropped my shovel.

"That's it. I'm out of here until they fix the light," I said aloud, trying to keep my voice calm. I had to stay calm. I reached out for the battery lantern but couldn't seem to grasp it. My hand was shaking so hard I had to drop the shovel and grab my wrist with my free hand to make it work. I most emphatically did not want to pick up the strobing lantern. But I did it and hurried down the tunnel toward the lift, forcing myself to walk slowly and calmly.

That's when I heard a sound behind me. Which was impossible. I had been working alone at the cave-in that blocked the end of the tunnel, and there certainly hadn't been anyone with me when the lights started strobing. So why did I hear footsteps behind me? It sounded as though someone were splashing their way through puddles of water. Which was ridiculous, because this tunnel was dry.

The lights were flickering off and on, off and on so fast they made my eyes sting. It was disorienting. I tried to ignore the sensation of cold eyes on the back of my head, to ignore the sound of footsteps walking behind me in a completely empty tunnel. But it was too much. The hairs all over my body rose straight up, and suddenly I whipped around to stare behind me into the dark tunnel. My flickering headlamp illuminated walls, ceiling, floor. There was nothing there.

At that moment, a bony finger poked my shoulder from behind. I gave a shriek and whirled around in the direction of the lift. And there, hanging before my eyes, were the withered head and torso of a man. It was floating a few feet above the ground, and in spite of the touch I'd felt on my shoulder, the specter had no arms or legs. Just a twisted head with wild hair, glowing eyes, and a mouth that broadened into an impossibly wide grin full of broken, yellow teeth. The shards of the teeth were so sharp they had cut right through the lips, leaving them in ghastly tatters. The eyes of the foul thing were just a few inches from my own.

I don't remember how long we stared at one another. I just remember suddenly sprinting past the leering creature, heading desperately for the lift and safety. I felt its deathly coldness as I squeezed past in the flickering light of the lantern, which had fallen from my hand at the sight of the specter. To my horror, the ghastly apparition kept pace with me as I ran. I could hear the feet it did not have pounding alongside my own.

I spotted the bell pull in the dim light of my flickering headlamp and summoned the lift with all my strength. As it rumbled to life and came shooting down toward four hundred feet, I chanced a look behind me and stared right into the glowing eyes of the specter. I screamed and lashed out at it and felt the hands it did not possess closing around my neck.

Suddenly, the lift was behind me, and I staggered into it, gasping and struggling against the strangling specter, only inches from my face. Grabbing for the bar of the lift, I ducked my head and lunged out with my foot, hitting the terrifying demon squarely in the chest. It was still grinning at me through tattered lips as it flew out of the lift and into the crazily strobing light of the battery lamp, lying on its side in the darkness of the tunnel.

"Up! Up!" I shouted frantically, closing the doors. A second later the hoist rumbled to life and the lift started rising. I lay panting on the floor and gazed down through the boards into the darkened, vertical shaft. And saw the torso of the creature floating underneath the lift. It stared up at me with malevolent eyes, and once again I felt invisible hands close around my throat and cut off my breath. I rolled and struggled, clawing frantically at my neck, trying to release the pressure, my eyes fixed on the specter below me. It kept up with the lift for nearly a hundred feet and then disappeared into a side shaft. At that moment, the pressure on my throat released and I gasped, desperately drawing breath into my starving lungs.

I lay like a dead man on the floor of the lift and couldn't move even when it reached the surface and a crowd of my fellow miners came scrambling over to help me. I guess I passed out then. The next thing I remember, I was lying in a hospital bed with bandages covering the terrible red welts on my neck, and a nurse was holding out a cool drink that soothed the pain in my throat.

They wanted me to talk about what happened down there, but every time I tried, my whole body seized up and started to tremble so bad I couldn't speak. Just to envision the specter was to feel the hands it didn't have closing around my throat. So I kept my mouth shut. As soon as I was able, I left the hospital, quit my job at the mine, and started working as a watchman. I never went underground again.

17

The Cowboy's Sweetheart

CUSTER COUNTY

I was having a good sulk that evening as I rode my horse home from the hoedown in old Johnston's barn. All the cowboys from the local ranches were there, and the townsfolk and the farmers too. It was a fabulous party, and I would have enjoyed it hugely if Alma Mae hadn't told me off earlier that afternoon. Bottom line, she wanted to settle down, and I didn't have enough money yet to support a wife. If she'd wait a year, I'd have enough saved to buy us a little farm. But she didn't want to wait a year, and she said so. Then she announced that she had decided to go to the party with Freddy Smith, who worked in town, and she flounced away over my protests.

Well, I was so down I didn't even want to go to the hoedown, but the other cowboys jeered at me until I got myself cleaned up and rode into town with the rest of them. The fiddler played and the caller sang, and everybody danced but me. I stood along the barn wall and glared at Alma Mae every time she whirled past with Fred.

Finally, I couldn't stand no more and stalked out of the barn. My horse was surprised to see me. She'd settled down to a good long nap and nipped crossly at my sleeve when I woke her. But she calmed down once we were out under that big Montana sky with a gibbous moon glowing above and about a million stars twinkling down on us. Around me, the wind sang softly through the prairie grass, and I could hear little night creatures zipping hither and thither as a few late-season crickets chirped. I calmed down as we meandered down the road toward the ranch, following the dip and flow of the land. It wasn't too long before I heard the river burbling ahead of me. I headed toward the ford and then pulled my horse to a stop abruptly as a figure came running suddenly up from the grove of trees near the bank. In the light of the moon, I saw it was a young woman in a soaking-wet dress. Her long hair was dripping and tangled around her face, and she looked desperately anxious.

"Oh, please sir, will you help me?" she cried, stopping at the edge of the road and gazing up at me with huge, dark eyes. She was extremely pretty. Much prettier than Alma Mae. And her whole body trembled in her distress.

I swung down off my horse immediately, removing my coat as I did so.

"Of course I'll help you, ma'am," I said, wrapping my coat around her shivering body. "What happened?"

"I think my horse heard a bear in the grove. It reared in midstream and threw me into the water. I . . . I had a bit of a disagreement with my sweetheart at the dance, and so I started for home early. But then my horse threw me, and now my head feels funny, and . . ." She almost fell over as she spoke. I steadied her and noticed a dark mark on her temple that her wet hair had covered when she first hurried up to the road.

"Come on," I said, lifting her up as easily as if she were a baby and sitting her on my horse. "I'll take you home. Where to?"

THE COWBOY'S SWEETHEART

She swayed a bit and put her hand to her head as I mounted behind her. But she roused a bit when I repeated my question and gave me directions to her home. She was a local girl who lived a few miles away from the ranch where I worked. I was surprised that I hadn't recognized her. I thought I knew all the girls from around here. After all, I'd been working at the ranch for over a year. I put the puzzle out of my mind for the moment and carefully crossed the river at the ford, keeping my ears open for the grunt of a bear. I heard nothing but the wind in the trees and the soft breathing of my companion. She was still shivering with cold, and her wet skirts were flapping against my legs and making me feel almost as wet and cold as she was.

I took the right fork instead of the left one and rode past farm after farm. This poor girl had come a long way to the dance, I mused. She was silent in my arms, except for the sound of her chattering teeth. "We're almost there," I said encouragingly as I turned my horse into the lane leading to her house. She nodded vaguely, as if she hadn't really heard me. I hoped the wound on her temple hadn't addled her wits.

As I rode toward the house, a man came out onto the porch carrying a lantern.

"I'm going to check on the hens, Mary. Something set them off," he called over his shoulder. Then he turned and saw us riding up the lane. His eyes went wide, and he dropped the lantern. In that instant, the girl in my arms disappeared.

I gave a gasp of shock, staring at the empty place where the girl had been just a second before. My heart started pounding heavily in my chest, and my stomach dropped right into my toes. I swear it did. My hands were shaking so hard I could barely rein in my horse.

I looked at the man on the porch, who was rescuing his fallen lantern. He was trembling too.

"Wh . . . what happened?" I managed to gasp over the beating of my heart. "Where did she go?"

The man rubbed a hand over his eyes and then gazed at me with terrible sadness in the flickering light of the lantern.

"That was my daughter. She died two years ago this evening. Her horse threw her into the river one night as she was riding home from a dance, and she hit her head and drowned."

I felt as if every nerve in my body was being squeezed by a giant hand. Cold shivers raced up and down my neck, and I broke out in a cold sweat. "That can't be," I protested. "She was right here. I know she was. She was completely solid. And look, my trousers are still wet from her dress!" I thrust a leg forward as I spoke and realized at that moment that my clothes were dry. My head started spinning, and only many years of horsemanship kept me in the saddle.

"This is some kind of joke," I said, pressing a hand to my forehead to stop the spinning sensation.

"No joke, lad," the man said heavily. "Come on, I'll show you. You can tie your horse to the porch rail."

Still feeling unsteady, I slid out of the saddle and tied up my mare. Then I followed him around the side of the house and across the yard. A big maple tree was standing in the corner by the fence. As we approached, the lantern lit the shadows underneath the tree, revealing a white gravestone. I gave a sudden cry and raced forward to drop to my knees in front of the stone. Draped across it was my jacket, the one I had wrapped around the girl to warm her after her fall in the river.

The man stood silently behind me, holding up his lantern so I could read the stone. It said: ALMA JANE MADDOCK, AGED 16. MAY SHE REST IN PEACE.

My heart thudded so hard in my chest I thought it would break a rib. Her name was Alma too. Just like my girl.

"You'd better take your jacket, son," the man said heavily. "And I want to thank you for helping our girl. She comes back sometimes, like tonight, looking for someone to save her. I'm obliged to you for trying."

I wanted to say something. Say anything to this heartbroken old man. But I couldn't force a word through my tight throat. Afraid that I might bawl like a baby, I nodded several times, retrieved my jacket, and went back to the house. A moment later I was on my horse and riding home.

All I could think of was Alma. Both Almas. And how I'd fought with my Alma a few hours before. Suddenly, I turned my horse and headed back toward the river. Back toward the dance. When I arrived, I swept my Alma right off Fred's arm, marched her out into the moonlight, and proposed. I even went down on one knee. I told her I'd give up wrangling and go to work in a shop to support her in style. Then Alma dropped down on *her* knees and started crying. Said she didn't want me to stop wrangling. She'd wait the year for me to buy the farm.

Wordless once again, I clutched her to my chest and kissed her. And kissed her again. She was warm and breathing and alive. And I would make her as happy as I could. Maybe, if I loved my Alma enough, it might make things up a little to that other Alma, who died in the river. Maybe.

18

The Party

The party was a roaring success. Roaring *being the key term at the moment,* the host thought blurrily as he downed another glass of whiskey. The sheer volume of the masses made his head ring. But at least everyone was having a good time. Perhaps a bit too good. If he didn't break apart some of those young people soon, their parents would come complaining to him in a few months. Not that he minded easy virtue. He practiced it himself.

The room was full of light, and the band was sawing away grandly while many of the country folk danced up and down the center of the room. Other couples were hiding away in corners doing heaven-alone knew what, though their host suspected they were behaving as badly as the young people. And the beer and wine and whiskey were flowing freely. *Now this,* he thought with a smile, *was exactly the way Lent should be celebrated every year.* If only Monsieur le Curé could see this lot! He'd tear out what little hair he had left, the old pious know-it-all.

The host frowned fiercely as he remembered the priest confronting him just the previous week. His reputation as a hard man was well earned. He beat his wife into submission, had sold

103

his only daughter into a life of sin, was brutal and miserly with the people who worked his ranch, and never attended church except on high holidays. If he didn't mend his ways, Monsieur le Curé said sternly, the Devil would come soon to take his soul away.

Mon Dieu, why was he thinking about the priest right now? It was spoiling the party mood, and over there was a sweet mademoiselle who had pouty red lips and a flirtatious air. His wife, hovering in the corner looking gray and worn and old, was completely ignored as the host made his way toward the pretty lady with the plunging neckline and the easy virtue. Nothing his wife said or did would have mattered to the host anyway, and years of being downtrodden kept her silent now, and watchful.

As the host took the lady's arm and led her into the dance, his wife turned aside in contempt and stared at the laughing, flirting, indecorous crowd. All of these people gave lip service to the church. They vowed to practice Lent in sobriety and propriety, as the good Monsieur le Curé had taught them. Yet look at them now! By day, they despised her husband as the worst of men; one who delighted in cruelty and pain. Her husband had killed more men in gunfights and spawned more vigilante hunts through the years than any other man in the territory. But by night, the story changed. Her husband was rich and powerful, and the country folk flocked to his parties for all the wine and debauchery they provided.

A fist fight broke out in the middle of the dance floor as two men came to blows over a flirtatious woman. Calmly, her husband pulled out his gun and shot both men—one in the heart, the other in the head. The band ground to a halt in a series of ear-numbing squeaks and whistles, and for a moment there was silence in the hall. Then the host nodded to two of his cowboys, who dragged out the bodies. The eyes of the sheriff met those of the host for a long moment. Then a serving maid handed the sheriff a big glass of whiskey and whispered suggestively in his ear. The sheriff turned away from the grisly scene, and the crowd sighed. "*Mes amis,* let us dance," their host shouted, waving for the music to continue. So they danced.

The despised, downtrodden little wife crept outside through the veranda doors of this house that was hers and yet not hers. She was sickened to her soul by such behavior. Was there no end to this torturous life? The priest had said he would pray for her salvation, but heaven seemed far away and unreal. She stared down the hill toward the dark waters of the pond as the moon rose blood-red over the horizon. The soft rustle of the wind in the prairie grasses and the lapping of the waves were the only sounds save the music. The night creatures were silent and still. No owl hooted. No black-footed ferret scrambled after a prairie dog meal. No cricket sang. No bat fluttered.

As she drew closer to the water, the uncanny stillness made her flesh creep. The water of the pond glowed red from the light of the moon. It looked like a lake of fire. And the smell was hot, steamy, and pungent. It made her nose twitch uneasily. It smelled like blood, pumped fresh from the artery of a dying man. Was this where the cowboys had brought the bodies of the dead? She stooped and dipped her hand into the water. And froze as it surged hot and thick and sticky against her fingers. *Mon Dieu.* It was blood!

At that moment, a great shout went up from the drunken revelers in the hall, and they came spilling out onto the lawn

THE PARTY

carrying lanterns that made them look like colorful fireflies. They were singing a French song that the downtrodden wife despised for its nasty, graphic lyrics. "A moonlight boat ride," she heard her husband calling out above the noise of the song. "You will ride with me, *ma petite chou.*" And she heard the mademoiselle giggle coyly as she clung to his arm.

His wife stared at her bloody hand. Then she scuttled sideways into the long grass of the field and ran as fast as she could away from the house toward the church where Monsieur le Curé lay awake, fasting and praying for those of his congregation who were, even then, breaking their Lenten vows.

As the host staggered drunkenly toward the pond with his party guests, a wave of heat laced with the hot stench of blood washed over them. The wind rose, rustling the prairie grasses. Very faintly, on the edge of hearing, came the sound of many voices screaming in agony. The wailing grew louder, higher pitched, until their ears buzzed and hurt. And the center of the lake burst into flames. Terrible, roaring flames they were, like the heart of a volcano. The bodies of dead fish rose to float on top of the lake in the light of the blood-red moon as the drunken party guests started to scream and trip over themselves running back up the hill. Many were trampled in the sudden stampede toward the house, and some were so drunk they fell over after taking a single step.

Two white-hot lines of fire came bursting forth from the maelstrom at the center of the lake of blood, running along either side of the lawn and meeting at the center of the veranda. The fence of flames rose higher and higher, pushing the fleeing guests back down toward the burning, churning, bloody lake. Out of the center of the red inferno stepped a tall, dark figure dressed in black with a blood-red cloak and hooves where his feet should have been. His eyes were the eyes of death, and the party guests went cold when they saw him, even though the night was steamy hot with the heavy stench of blood and flames.

With a scream of terror that equaled the wailing, screeching voices in the wind, one man went running up the slope of the hill and flung himself at the fence of fire. At once, he was encased in flames, burning horribly before the eyes of the other guests. His terrible screams turned into a soft, continuous wailing like the cry of a baby as he burned to death before their eyes. In a moment, the wailing had ceased and all that was left was a small pile of gray ashes. The dark figure at the center of the lake laughed as he died.

"Stop!" A clear voice came ringing out from the far side of the flames. Instantly, every party guest went silent as they recognized the voice of their priest. A small stream of holy water rose up over the blazing white fence of fire, and where it hit, the fire went out. Monsieur le Curé stepped onto the lawn and gazed down at his impious, debauched congregants, and then out across the blood-red lake to the figure standing just above the churning surface. Beside him, the downtrodden wife stood panting and praying, tears streaming down her face as the wails on the wind took on a new sobbing sound, like the souls of lost infants. "Come to me, my children," the priest called with sorrow and compassion in his clear voice. "Come to me."

Above the waters of the lake, the dark figure stood motionless as one after another, the men and women on the lawn stumbled to their feet and walked toward the priest. He touched each head with a drop of holy water and then sent them through the door in the flames. But as the host turned to follow his guests, the dark figure on the blood-red lake spoke. "No!" it thundered. "No. Those two are mine."

The Devil pointed at the murdering, cheating man who stood trembling on the lakeshore, one arm still wrapped around the waist of the drunken mademoiselle. Monsieur le Curé gave a little nod. And the flaming maelstrom at the center of the lake rose up in fury, encompassing the whole lake, the Devil, and the wicked man and woman standing on the shore. The flaming fence rose as high as the roof of the house, spitting and sizzling and cooking the skin of all those who had not yet received a drop of holy water on their forehead. And then the fire went out as suddenly as it had appeared, and the moon turned white and serene overhead.

The guests crept home, sober and scared to death. Those who had been singed in the last fiery surge paused only long enough to receive a drop of holy water over their reddened faces before scurrying away with the rest. And Monsieur le Curé performed a blessing over the ranch house and all who worked there on the shores of the lake before sending them to their beds.

The country folk never broke their Lenten vows again, and the whole community was soon held up as a model town in all the surrounding territory. As for the downtrodden wife, she located her poor, lost daughter and brought her home. And the ranch became a happy place at last.

Faster!

VIRGINIA CITY

A man like Jack Slade didn't deserve her. Of that I was morally certain. Jack Slade was a drunkard. Jack Slade was a gunslinger. Jack Slade had murdered twenty-six men during his career with the Overland Stage Company, and he carried the dried ears of a man he tortured to death on his watch chain. Jack Slade vandalized property every time he came to drink in Virginia City. And Jack Slade was married to the woman I wanted more than I wanted my own salvation.

Virginia Slade was a fine-looking woman, yes, sir. But it wasn't her looks that had captured my heart. Virginia had more fire and gumption than any gal I'd ever met. I'd fallen head over heels for her at first sight. I remember it like yesterday. She was striding down the boardwalk in Virginia City, giving Jack Slade a piece of her mind for wasting his money on drink. Her eyes were flashing with fire and passion, and she waved her dainty hands so expressively my heart started thumping in my chest at the sight. Jack was nearly sober at the time and was laying it on thick about how he would change his ways, all out of love for her. But she wasn't buying any of it.

FASTER!

A few moments later, they were in the wagon and heading north on the toll road where they'd built their home. I watched them ride out of sight, knowing I'd do anything to possess Virginia Slade. But what could I do? I'm a pretty fair hand with a gun, but Jack was better. And it became swiftly apparent that Virginia had eyes only for her man, in spite of his being a devil.

So I bided my time, ran my store, and panned for gold on the side, patiently awaiting my moment. Jack Slade made enemies as easily as other folks made friends. Sooner or later, his end would come. And I would do everything I could to promote that end. So I watched as Jack Slade rolled boisterously from one saloon to the next, shooting up each place as he got drunk. Before the end of his first month in Virginia City, there wasn't a store owner or saloon manager who didn't have one of Jack's bullet holes in his ceiling, business sign, water barrel, or bar top. I took particular pleasure in fanning the flames of resentment in the men whose property he regularly defaced. And of course, he got into huge rows with the other drunkards in the bar, making still more enemies as time went on. Then Jack started riding through town with his drunken friends, all of them shooting and yelling like devils, firing their revolvers, riding their horses into stores, and destroying the goods within. That didn't sit at all well with the community.

For all his roistering and fiery arguing, Jack never escalated any of his drunken rows into a gunfight. To my intense frustration, he never killed a man in town. If he'd murdered just one man, I'd have had him. But he stayed on the straight and narrow in this regard, at least. The infamous gunslinger and murderer was changing, and it had to be due to his lovely, spirited wife. Why else would he mend his ways? It was frustrating in the extreme to see the woman I wanted so close to me and yet so far away. Strolling down the streets of Virginia City on the arm of a man like Jack Slade.

Mind you, I was also working on Virginia Slade. I spoke to her every time she came to town, engaging her lively mind on all manner of genteel topics, and making careful note of her likes and dislikes. I was both shocked and delighted to learn she was nearly as good a shot with a pistol as her no-good husband. She tossed her dark head proudly when she made this boast, and I challenged her to a shooting contest right then and there. We lined cans up on a fencepost and shot them off at twenty paces. She knocked off every can, slick as a whistle, and she was so fast she even shot up a couple of mine before I could get to them. What a woman!

Then my luck changed. Folks in both Nevada City and Virginia City were fed up with the lawless behavior of the gold miners and the other reckless men, and they wanted justice. A lawyer named Wilbur F. Sanders formed a vigilance committee that was more than eager to uphold the law. This was my chance. Jack Slade's days were numbered!

The vigilantes were everything I'd hoped they would be. They dispensed justice without mercy, not just hunting down murderers, but also men whose crimes were not so heinous. Justice was swift and usually ended in the noose, and in the vigilantes' fervor, they hung more than one man to appease the public's sense of justice, whether or not he actually deserved it. This fit in very well with my plans. Sooner or later, Jack Slade would do something that outraged the public. And then I would have him!

It turned out to be sooner, and his crime was more of a practical joke than anything else. Jack and a couple of his cronies got roaring drunk one night, shot up a local milk wagon, and then pushed it over a hill. Milk spilled everywhere and the wagon was destroyed. This was it. I knew it in my bones. Folks in Nevada and Virginia Cities would be deprived of fresh milk for days because of Jack Slade. And they were not going to be happy about it. I spread the rumor far and wide, encouraging every angry comment, every voice that raised itself against Jack Slade. A warrant was issued for his arrest for disturbing the peace. It was said that Jack tore it to pieces and swore vengeance on the judge who'd issued it.

In fact, Jack was so angry that he came to town in a reckless rage, looking for the judge. He was confronted by a couple of his friends, who urged him to go home. I made sure I was one of them, so when the time came, Virginia would not blame me for his death. But on his way out of town, he spotted the judge and began a tirade against him. He was still yelling and cussing when a posse of miners came into town to arrest him. Jack was tried and convicted then and there. The sentence? Death by hanging.

No sooner was he convicted of the crime than Jack was dragged to a gallows. I stayed in the background, watching with glee. What I did not anticipate was that friends of Jack would ride swiftly down the toll road to tell Virginia what was happening. Even as Jack was marched to the gallows and the noose tightened around his neck, the sound of a pistol firing again and again came from the north. I turned and saw a wild-eyed woman, black hair whipping frantically in the wind stirred up by her galloping horse, riding as fast as she could down the hill toward town.

"Faster, faster!" Virginia screamed at her horse, and she fired her pistol at anyone and anything that stood in her way. I glanced back toward the gallows in time to see the executioner kick the crate out from under Jack's feet. By the time Virginia reached town, he was dead. With a scream of agony, Virginia slid down from the saddle. Tears streamed across her lovely face as she stared at the husband she had loved so foolishly but so well. Then she whirled into the street, pistol in hand. Her rage was so fierce that everyone in the mob took a step back, and many hurriedly found business elsewhere.

Many a vigilante or a townsperson heard the sharp side of Virginia's tongue that day. So abusive was she that some of the men threatened to string her up too if she didn't get out of town immediately with Jack's body. Disdainful, spirited as ever, and so angry she couldn't speak, Virginia took her dead husband home to her ranch and refused to have him buried in this benighted territory. Instead, she filled his coffin with whiskey and shipped his body to Salt Lake City to be buried there when the snow melted.

The next few weeks were tense. Somehow, Virginia discovered the names of the men primarily responsible for Jack's death sentence, and she made their lives miserable. As a "friend" who had supported Jack in his last hour, I was looked upon with gratitude and friendship. And I was quick to play upon that friendship. After a decent interval, I started courting the lovely widow in earnest. And won her heart! It was the happiest day of my life when she became my wife.

I don't know who it was that told her the truth about me. If I ever find out, I will kill him. One day, she was laughing and loving and sweet. The next silent and thoughtful. And then she was gone, leaving only a note behind accusing me of killing her Jack. And that was that. I received formal notice of divorce a couple of years after she left.

It turned me bitter, I confess. I'd loved her with all my soul and had freed her from her monster of a husband. And she'd left me. Frankly, I was glad to see the last of her, and never once did I repent of my actions against Jack Slade. I was well rid of them both.

Time passed, as it has a habit of doing, and Virginia married another. Good riddance to bad rubbish, I thought, hardening my heart against her. And I was still immovable when reports of her death came to my ears.

Until one moonlit night, when I came stumbling out of one of the local saloons. I was a little worse for drink and feeling melancholy as I staggered toward my horse, thinking about the empty, loveless house that was my abode. At that moment, the wind died suddenly, leaving the night still and empty. No creature stirred. No owl hooted. It was the stillness of death and the grave, and it made my blood run cold. I realized suddenly that I was alone on the street. Too alone.

I turned in fear toward the comfort of the saloon behind me, where the bartender still polished his glasses and one or two men still nursed their whiskey. And stopped when I heard the frantic pounding of hooves coming from just northeast of town. Coming down the old toll road. In a flash, I remembered a day long ago when the vigilantes were stringing up a rowdy gunslinger for disturbing the peace. And I saw now, as I had seen then, a figure racing frantically toward town. This figure was glowing white from within, her hair blowing every which way as she fired her pistol to disburse the crowd in front of her. Her horse was moving faster than any living creature ever could. And the terrible fear and anger on her face shook me to the core. A deep, guttural moaning rose up through the earth and burst forth into the air. The ground shook with it, and the trees bent under its weight. It was heard as much in the bone as by the ear, and I fled before it, my legs turning my body around even before my mind registered the motion.

The sound rose higher and higher in pitch, mixed with the terrible pounding of hooves as the horse and its rider swept down upon me. I couldn't outrun them. Nothing could. The moaning noise made my brain throb, and I clapped my hands to my ears, which were already trickling with blood. Still, the agonized moaning grew louder and higher in pitch. My stomach heaved, and my brain felt as if it were exploding under the sound. I whirled around to face the galloping figure. For a moment, the whole world turned white as the phantom swept right through my body. Then I pitched face forward onto the ground, and my very last thought was of poor Jack Slade.

20

Crop Circle

WIBAUX COUNTY

I stood proudly next to a tall stalk of corn in the twilight, looking down the long, narrow rows of my crop. It was the first year I had tried to grow feed corn for my cattle, and I had a bumper crop ready to harvest within the week. Not bad at all for an experiment! I'd hoped to reduce some of my costs by raising my own feed, and it looked like I would succeed.

I heard the rattle of a passing wagon, and three voices yelled a greeting. I looked up and waved as Sylvia, my daughter-in-law, drove past with my two grandsons. They were on their way to her parents' house for the weekend. That meant my eldest son Tim—who helped me run the ranch—was baching it this weekend. He'd be over soon to have supper with us, I was sure. Tim can't cook!

I was humming happily to myself as I skirted the field and headed in toward the house, pausing quickly to wash my hands at the pump in the yard before making my way to the kitchen. I could smell fried chicken. My favorite!

Melissa was mashing up potatoes when I entered the room. My wife was as pretty and rosy cheeked now as when I'd first carried her over the threshold thirty years ago. She looked too young to have three grown children and a couple of grands. Not like me! I'd gotten brown and wrinkled from the sun, and my eyes were a tad too narrow from squinting out over the backs of the cattle as we shifted them around the range.

"How's the corn?" she asked, placing a steaming bowl of mashed potatoes on the table beside the fried chicken. I sniffed appreciatively.

"Ready to harvest. I'll ask Tim to bring the harvester over tomorrow and help me bring in the crop."

"Speaking of our eldest, where is Tim?" Melissa asked, glancing out the window. "I told him we were having chicken. You'd have thought he'd come running." Fried chicken was Tim's favorite dish.

She was answered by the sound of hoofbeats echoing down the lane. A moment later, Tim's horse was tied up to our hitching post, and the excited clump of feet stomping up the back steps heralded the entrance of my eldest.

"Whoo-ee, that crop of corn is looking fine, Pop," he said, bussing his mother on the cheek, grabbing a plate from the cupboard, and helping himself to chicken. "I was thinking we could hitch the horses to the harvester tomorrow and bring in the crop."

That set off a spate of talk about the whys and wherefores of harvesting corn, something that was new to both of us. Melissa just smiled and kept passing around the food. We offered Tim a bed for the night, but he refused, saying he had livestock to tend. After we all devoured one of my wife's apple pies, Melissa and I went out onto the porch and watched Tim riding down the lane toward his house, which was a half mile away from ours. It was one of those gorgeous nights you get in late summer. The soft breeze was filled with the scent of the climbing roses that grew up the trellis by the porch, and the air was filled with the chirp of crickets. We sat on the steps, staring up at the endless, star-studded sky and holding hands. I smiled as I looked out over my cornfields. I could hear the occasional soft lowing of the cattle as they settled down for the night. All was peaceful.

We drifted to bed eventually and snuggled in for the night only to be shocked awake after midnight when a bright light abruptly blazed into our bedroom. I'd never seen such a blinding light. It brought me upright mighty quick. A huge blast of wind shook the house as I staggered to my feet, Melissa right behind me. We raced to the window and saw something huge, flat, and round as a pancake land dead center in the cornfield, blasting my crop every which way. My cornfield!

Outside, the horses were racing around and around the paddock in sheer panic, and the milk cows milled about and mooed in fear in the close pasture. I cursed aloud, dragged on my trousers, and ran downstairs to get my gun. Outside, the noise and the light faded, but I could still hear the animals panicking.

"Henry, be careful!" Melissa shouted to me. "You don't know what that thing is!"

"I know it's ruining my feed corn!" I roared in sheer rage, grabbing my rifle and running down the lawn and into the cornfield. I was racing along one of the narrow rows of corn when I smashed headlong into a wall of dark metal and bounced backward, falling onto my bottom, the rifle clutched foolishly in both hands.

Jehoshaphat! Whatever it was, it was huge! The metal pancake towered a good twenty feet above my head. I stood up and felt the side of it. It was smooth and silky to the touch, not like any metal I've ever felt. And it purred under my hand like a kitten, though I heard no sound.

Suddenly, Melissa screamed from the direction of the barn. My heart nearly stopped at the sound, and I was running before I was even aware of it, crashing straight through the corn and doing nearly as much damage as the strange metal object in the field.

"Melissa! I'm coming!" I shouted, and let off a volley of shots into the air to frighten off whatever was menacing her.

I heard a couple of answering shots, and realized my spunky wife had armed herself with the spare rifle before heading out to check on the animals. As I burst forth from the tall cornstalks that were blocking my view, I heard hooves pounding down the lane from the main road and Tim shouting: "Mama! Pop! What's going on!" He must have seen the light from his house and come hurrying to the rescue.

"Help me find your mother," I yelled to him as I raced toward the barn. He beat me there by a whisker, swinging off his horse and leaping straight through the double doors just as we heard Melissa shouting: "Stay away from our horses, whatever you are! Stay away or I'll shoot!"

Her voice was coming from the paddock. I leapt over the fence in a bound I couldn't have bettered as a boy, raced around the side of the barn, and stopped dead still at the sight of a tall, black cloud of vapor pouring itself through the barn door. It was thick like fog and blacker than the darkness. Slowly it formed a tall column, and where it swirled, it obscured the stars. The horses were all pressed against the fence, as far from the swirling column as they could get, and Melissa was standing on

CROP CIRCLE

the lowest rail beside the panting horses, her rifle trained on the dark column.

I could hear Tim in the barn, cursing at some unseen foe within. "Stay away from my mother!" he shouted, his voice echoing strangely inside the big building.

After a moment, I could make out what appeared to be a few glowing figures inside the black mist. Grimly, I aimed my gun at them and stalked forward. "Get off my property right now or I'll shoot," I said.

"Henry, don't you walk into that fog," Melissa said. I'd never heard such a ferocious tone from my mild-tempered wife. It stopped me in my tracks. The last of the dark fog flowed out of the doorway, and Tim followed it. He'd grabbed a third rifle from the tack room, so we were all armed now.

"I said: Get off my property," I repeated, taking aim at the nearest glow inside the swirling column of darkness. And then I was blown completely off my feet by a sudden, huge blast of air from the cornfield. Immediately, the horses screamed and reared. One jumped the fence right beside Melissa, knocking her to the ground. The others raced around the paddock, steering clear of the black column. I scrambled hastily out of their way as the same brilliant light that had awakened us blazed out from the metal pancake, which was rising slowly out of the cornfield. The fierce wind it produced flattened my feed corn to the ground, which made me furious all over again.

"Mama!" shouted Tim, seeing Melissa fall off the fence. He ran right through the dark column of mist, brushing aside one of the glowing figures in his haste to reach my wife. Melissa was already scrambling to her feet by the time he reached her.

Seeing that my wife was all right, I advanced on the

invaders. "*Get out now!*" I screamed at them, and shot my rifle in their midst. The dark cloud obscured my view of them, but the message was clear. Misty black cloud and glowing figures moved with unnatural speed back through the barn door. I followed at their heels and saw them burst out the double front doors and race off across the fields, gaining height and speed so rapidly that in the end it was like watching the reverse of a shooting star. The blackness streaked out over the pastures like a bullet, a blackness relieved in spots by a few glowing forms. Then it vanished over the horizon. Hovering above the cornfield, the metal pancake suddenly quenched its lights and went streaking up and away in the opposite direction from the black mist.

I ran back to my wife and son, who were kneeling together on the ground, staring at the cornfield. "That thing," Tim gasped as I gathered my wife into my arms to make sure she was all right. "That thing could fly! Just like a bird."

"Both of those things," I corrected grimly. "That black misty thing took off into the air just like that pancake did."

"I thought it looked more like a saucer," my son joked feebly.

"Flying pancake, flying saucer. Whatever. It's gone now. Are you all right?" I asked my wife.

"Fine," she said, her voice muffled against my shoulder. "I'm just plumb mad at those varmints. Look what they've done to our cornfield."

We all turned to look at the corn. In the moonlight, we saw a giant circle pressed into the center of the field where all the cornstalks had been flattened by the metal pancake. I groaned when I saw it. But Tim patted my shoulder comfortingly. "We'd be knocking down the corn anyway tomorrow to harvest it. We can probably save some of it," he said.

I looked at him closely in the moonlight. "Are you all right?" I belatedly asked my son. "You ran right through that darkness!"

"It felt like fog," Tim said, shrugging off the experience with a casualness that didn't deceive me in the least. I could see he was shaking. "I knocked into a figure that looked like a glowing scarecrow. It's clothes were shiny and puffy looking, as if they'd been stuffed with hay, and it had a glowing round ball where its head should be. Strange!"

I nodded. "Let's get your mother to the house," I said, rising carefully to my feet with my wife still clasped in my arms. I wasn't about to let her go. We made our way slowly back to the house. Tim's horse had disappeared; probably panicked when the metal pancake rose from the field. We'd have to search for it and the other escapee in the morning.

The warmth and sanity of daylight came as a blessed relief from the crazy events of the night. Tim and I rose early and went to look for the missing horses. Old Nelly, who'd jumped the paddock fence, was grazing by the barn, but Tim's horse remained missing. We finally gave up and went to do the morning chores. Over breakfast, we discussed the matter in depth.

"It must have been some new-fangled invention like the steam train or the motor car," Melissa said as she served us pancakes dripping with butter and maple syrup.

"I think we'd have heard about it if someone had invented a flying machine," I said, eyeing the pancakes suspiciously.

"Creatures from another world," Tim speculated, wolfing down pancakes and bacon as fast as he could swallow. "Or one of them crazy inventions like that fellow Jules Verne is always writing about."

Melissa's eyes got round and excited: "*From Earth to the Moon*! That's the name of one of his books. Maybe they were moon men!"

I snorted derisively and decided to eat my pancakes. They weren't made of metal, after all, and they smelled delicious. "Probably some government experiment," I said, swallowing a large mouthful. "I wish I could charge them for my ruined corn!"

When we were done eating, Tim and I went outside to assess the damage to the corn crop. Much of the field was still intact, but the corn in the circle where the pancake had landed was completely crushed. Still, it was worth hitching the horses to the harvester and bringing the rest of it in.

Tim walked back to his house to get the new harvester, and I saddled up Nelly and had another ride around the ranch, looking for his horse. I found it half hidden on the far edge of the cornfield. It was dead and lay on its side, glassy eyed. There was no apparent reason for its death. Not a bone was broken, as far as I could see. Tim's saddle lay a few feet away from the horse's body. It had been carefully dragged out of sight among the corn stalks, as if someone had wanted to hide it. I frowned, realizing that there had probably been more invaders than we realized; perhaps a second black cloud filled with glowing figures had stolen Tim's horse while we were busy in the paddock. That made me wonder about the beef cattle I had pastured in one of the outlying fields. I'd only checked on the milk cows this morning. I swung up on Nelly and galloped out to the beef cattle in the far pasture. And yes, four of them were down, dead for no apparent reason. They formed a small circle, their heads at the center with horns stuck in the dirt and their bodies stretched out flat.

I was grim-faced and solemn when Tim drove up on the new harvester behind his two mammoth workhorses. I told him about his horse and the dead cattle, and we decided that we needed to do a postmortem on the animals to see what had killed them. As if we didn't already know. We put the harvester in the barn, saddled the workhorses to the wagon, and fetched the bodies from the far pasture and the cornfield. Then we spent the rest of the day examining the dead animals. It was creepy. None of them had a drop of blood left inside them. Not one. And every internal organ was missing. Yet there was no cut or abrasion on their skin. So how had their blood and organs been removed?

By the time we finished our grisly task, it was dusk. Neither of us wanted the dead animals anywhere near our ranch, so we hitched up the wagon again and drove them out into the wilderness and dumped them. Then we went home. Melissa had lit every lantern in the place, and the house looked warm and welcoming as we drove up the lane.

"Do you think they'll come back?" Tim asked nervously as we pulled up in front of the barn.

"They'd better not," I said, fingering my rifle.

"I don't think we can tell anyone about this," Tim said, halting the horses by the door and climbing down.

"Who'd believe us?" I agreed. "I hardly believe it myself."

We unhitched the horses, rubbed them down, and put them in the barn along with the wagon. Then we went inside to supper.

Tomorrow, we'd forget all about mysterious objects that dropped out of the sky and we'd bring in the corn crop. But I swore to myself that if any more metal pancakes landed in the night, I'd give the moon men such a licking they'd never come near my ranch again.

21

Rubberoo

BILLINGS

"Oh, Etienne, I almost forgot. We will be having a guest for dinner," Margaret said, looking up from her knitting. She was seated by the fire, which made a soft golden halo around her blond hair. In the dancing firelight, her face looked guileless and sweet.

Etienne looked up from his newspaper and frowned at his wife of twenty-five years. She knew he did not like surprises. She smiled at him warmly, and he relaxed a little, basking in her obvious adoration. And why shouldn't she adore him? He was an important attorney, a rich man, and he was thinking of running for mayor. He, in turn, was proud of his lovely wife. He had worked very hard to win her hand, and he deserved to bask now in her love.

"Who are we having to dinner, my dear?" he asked.

"An old friend of yours from Montreal," Margaret said with a happy smile. "Jean-Claude Dubois!"

Etienne started imperceptibly at the name and his eyes narrowed. But Margaret babbled on in sunny innocence: "I met him in front of the mercantile this afternoon. He had just arrived in town and had no fixed engagements, so I invited him to take dinner with us. He hasn't changed a bit since the last time I saw him. Remember? When he came with you to my coming-out dance?"

Oh, yes. Etienne remembered that day very well. Very well indeed. It was the day her former betrothed, Lucas, had been savagely killed by a rogue wolf on his way to the coming-out ball. Margaret and Lucas had planned to announce their engagement at the party. It has been a sad day for Margaret. And a happy one for Etienne. He remembered being impressed when Jean-Claude, his "friend" from Montreal, had arrived on time for the party, not a hair out of place or a wrinkle in his suit to declare what his business had been out there on a dark, empty road only a few minutes before the first dance was announced.

Before he could utter a word, the butler appeared in the doorway, announcing their guest. Etienne and Margaret rose as a suave, dark-haired man strolled into the room and bowed elegantly to them both. Margaret hurried forward, hands outstretched, and Jean-Claude kissed them one at a time before turning and offering Etienne a firm handshake.

"Jean-Claude," Etienne said, waving him to a seat. "How interesting to see you again. May I offer you a drink?"

Jean-Claude smoothly accepted and sat down on the settee beside Margaret.

"What brings you to Montana, *mon ami?*" Etienne asked, handing him a sherry and pouring another for his wife.

"I have family business in Butte with the copper kings," Jean-Claude said, shipping his sherry. "And other business takes me to British Columbia when I am done in Montana."

Etienne's glass shook a little as he recalled just what Jean-Claude's family business was. Assassinating. They were all assassins, and such was their skill and so unusual their gifts that no one in the United States or Canada would ever be able to convict them even if they could catch them in the act.

"Will you be staying long in town?" he asked, taking his former seat across from the settee.

"This is a mere stopover on my way to Butte," Jean-Claude purred gently. "It was an unsought pleasure to meet your charming wife outside the mercantile. I had no idea you were still living in Montana. Indeed, I had not realized you had wed one another until the lovely Madam Baptiste told me her married name."

He smiled suavely at Margaret, who pinked happily, threw her husband a loving glance, and took a sip of her sherry.

"I will never forget your kindness to me at my coming-out party," Margaret said shyly. "Do you remember, Etienne? That strange old railroad man accosted me in the garden, shouting out about rubberoos and waving his whiskey bottle around? If Jean-Claude hadn't stopped him, I don't know what might have happened!"

"I was happy to be of service to such a lovely lady," Jean-Claude said, placing a hand over his heart and bowing. Etienne frowned at such flamboyant behavior, but Margaret seemed to be enjoying it.

The butler appeared in the doorway and announced dinner. They all rose, and Jean-Claude took Margaret's arm and escorted her through to the dining parlor. Over dinner, they discussed politics, the settlement of the Montana territory, and the latest news from Montreal, where both Jean-Claude and Etienne had grown up. Etienne relaxed a little as the meal progressed. It was silly to be on edge. The contract that had originally brought the assassin to this town was finished long ago, on the night of the coming-out party, and no one had been the wiser. Jean-Claude's visit to town twenty-five years later was a coincidence, nothing more.

As they were eating dessert, Jean-Claude inquired after any children they might have. Etienne glared at him. How dare he bring up such a painful topic? Etienne had cast his only child out six months ago, unbeknownst to his mother. The cover story he'd told his wife was that the boy wanted to see the world before settling down to a career, and so he had started off on a grand tour of the United States with his father's blessing. But the truth was that Etienne had sent the defiant child away with barely a cent in his pocket to survive as best he could on his own. And he'd intercepted the letter his son had written to his mother, so Margaret never knew of the breach. He wanted Margaret to forget they ever had such a disobedient son, and the boy's sudden death had come as something of a relief. Now here was Jean-Claude, bringing up a subject that could only cause his wife more pain.

Before Etienne could interject, Margaret answered the assassin: "We had one son. Jonathan. He was making a grand tour of America, but he died in a freak accident while visiting one of the mines in Butte earlier this year." Her lovely blue eyes filled with tears at the memory.

"Madame, I grieve with you," Jean-Claude said, reaching over to take Margaret's hand.

Etienne was furious. If looks could kill, Jean-Claude would have dropped dead in his seat. *Take your hands off my wife,* he wanted to scream at the assassin. But politeness held his tongue. After all, the uncomfortable meal was almost over, the assassin would be gone forever, and he and Margaret would go back to their peaceful existence.

They lingered long over dessert and still longer in the parlor. Etienne grew sullen and impatient, but neither Jean-Claude nor Margaret seemed to notice. They talked and laughed together until the hour grew late, and the assassin finally rose to take his leave.

"No, Madame, stay in your comfortable seat by the warm fire," Jean-Claude said to Margaret. "*Mon ami* Etienne will see me safely on my way. And God bless you, Madame."

Margaret smiled at the assassin who—had she but known it—had killed her betrothed, and bade him a fond farewell. And then Etienne and Jean-Claude were out in the hallway. The assassin said: "*Mon ami,* walk with me to the gate, *s'il vous plait.*"

Etienne glanced nervously about, but the butler was nowhere to be seen. Reluctantly, he agreed. The two men shrugged on overcoats and scarves and walked out into the chilly, wind-swept night. Snow was deeply packed on either side of the shoveled brick walkway, and it mounded up so high near the street that the wrought-iron fence around the property was barely visible. The two men paused at the fence, and Jean-Claude said softly: "So it worked, *mon ami.* You hired me to kill Margaret's betrothed on the very night of her coming-out dance, and then you stepped into his shoes. I ask you now: Was it worth it? *Non,* you do not have to answer. One look at the lovely face of your wife says that it was. But what is the story with your son, I wonder?"

Etienne glared at him in the dim light reflected off the snow. "The boy was a disaster. Always in trouble. Always making up to his mother. Spending money recklessly. Drinking. Defying me.

Me, his father! So I sent him away. And he got himself killed in a cave-in in the mines. That is all."

"So abrupt you are, *mon ami*," Jean-Claude said lightly. "Do you not like talking to me? After all, we are old friends! And like all old friends, we share an old, old secret. Come, walk me to my hotel."

Etienne shivered then and hung back. "I'd rather not," he said. "Margaret will miss me."

"She will know where you have gone," Jean-Claude said, taking his arm in a grip of steel and pulling him through the gate onto the sidewalk. "Come, Etienne, how can a powerful man such as yourself be nervous walking with me? After all, I am only a . . . what was it the old railroad man called me? Ah, yes. I am only a rubberoo! Besides, I kill only by contract. What have you to fear from me?"

That was true, Etienne remembered. The assassin did have a code of honor—howbeit a strange one. He fell into step beside Jean-Claude Dubois, feeling relieved. Around them, the gas lamps made puddles of light on the icy streets. The wind was so cold it bit right through Etienne's coat and made him shudder. The assassin seemed to feel nothing.

"I made just the one mistake that night so long ago," Jean-Claude mused as they walked the midnight streets, through the whistling, jostling wind. "I let myself be seen by that drunken old railroad conductor as I was changing form. The stink of a passing steam train masked his scent from me. Before I could do anything about him, young Lucas was in sight and I had a paid contract to perform. By the time the boy was dead, the old man had disappeared into the station. It was sheer bad luck that the man knew Margaret and came to warn her about me.

Fortunately, she did not understand him, and I was able to silence him permanently later that evening."

Etienne was mesmerized by the assassin's voice. The world had narrowed into an icy dream lit by the occasional street lamp. But the lights were getting fewer and farther apart, and suddenly Etienne realized that they were not heading toward the hotel at all. They were walking along a vacant side street that bordered the railroad tracks. It was the same side street where Lucas's savaged body had been discovered twenty-five years ago.

"Silenced him permanently?" he asked, shaking with cold and sudden fear. "I thought you only killed for money."

"Oh, I didn't kill the railroad conductor," Jean-Claude purred. "No, I paid him many pieces of gold to forget what he'd seen. And so he left town and started life over again in Butte." Jean-Claude paused and placed a hand on Etienne's arm.

Jean-Claude swung the suddenly trembling attorney to face him, and in the snow-filled night, the assassin's eyes glowed red. "Where, twenty-five years later, he met Jonathan, your despised and rejected son. He told the boy all about the rubberoo who had been hired to kill his mother's fiancé so that you could marry her."

Jean-Claude's voice was changing. It had grown deeper, and there was the growl of a wolf in it. Etienne felt the nails on the hand clutching his arm grow longer and sharper, cutting through the material of his coat.

"It was your son's wish that his despised father should face the same fate as Lucas. As he lay broken and perishing from his wounds in the charity hospital in Butte, Jonathan Baptiste begged the old railroad conductor to put out a contract on his father, Etienne Baptiste, and to pay the assassin who killed Lucas

RUBBEROO

to fulfill it. I have in my pocket a letter from your son to his mother, telling her the whole story, which I mean to deliver to Margaret in the morning. And who knows? Maybe it is my turn to comfort the grieving widow!" The last word ended in a growl as Jean-Claude transformed from a suavely handsome man into a huge, gray wolf. *Loup garou*. Rubberoo. The perfect assassin. With the last ounce of his humanity, Jean-Claude howled one word: "Run!"

And Etienne ran, stumbling and sliding, down an icy street where a young man named Lucas—handsome, laughing, and very much in love—had come face to face with a *loup garou* twenty-five years before. As then, so now—neither man stood a chance.

22

Grizzly

PARK COUNTY

I was carefully packing flies into my tackle box when my wife strolled into the garage to admire my brand-new fly rod.

"Where are you headed today?" Cheryl asked after minutely inspecting my new rod. My wife is an enthusiastic supporter of my favorite hobby, which is one of the many reasons why I married her.

"I'm heading down to the Yellowstone River," I told her, holding up a fancy new fly for her inspection. Cheryl's eyes widened, and it took me a moment to realize she was reacting to my choice of destination, not my new fly.

"Oh, honey, I'm not comfortable with that," Cheryl said. "I've heard they're having a real problem with grizzlies along the Yellowstone this fall."

I'd heard that too, but discounted it. Every year brought stories about wild grizzlies, and if I heeded them all, I'd never fish again.

"I'll be extra careful," I said, showing her the small bear bells I had sewn onto my fly-fishing vest. Cheryl didn't look convinced, but she didn't argue with me. She'd delivered her warning, and if I was too stubborn to heed it, then so be it. She kissed me goodbye and watched as I climbed into the truck and headed out to my favorite fishing spot along the river.

It was a beautiful day for a drive. The mountain peaks were already dusted with snow, but the air was fair and warm. A perfect day for fishing. I sang happily to myself as I drove: "Camptown ladies, sing this song, doo-dah, doo-dah!" It was my Grandpa Dennis's favorite song. We'd sung it together every time we went fly-fishing. Grandpa had died three years ago now, and I missed him most on fishing days, when I went alone to the streams and rivers we used to visit together.

I parked in my usual spot just off the road and pulled out my fishing gear, warbling tunefully: "Camptown race track, five miles long, oh, doo-dah day." I slung my rod over my shoulder and started making my way through the trees and bracken toward the old fishing hole. It was a bit of a trek from my parking spot, but I always enjoyed the hike. And the hole wasn't so well known to the other anglers, which was a bonus.

"Gonna run all night, gonna run all day . . . " I sang, stepping over a log and rounding a corner. The river came in sight. So did the grizzly. I stopped in midwarble, frozen in my tracks. The bear looked up sharply from its place on the bank and stared right at me. For a moment, I stared back in shock. It was huge. Enormous. It had to be at least seven feet long, and it had a large hump over its brown shoulders and powerful hind legs. The head was large and round with a concave facial profile, and its coat was tipped with silver. Definitely a grizzly. As for the claws . . . well, they looked long and sharp. This was not good.

Quick as a flash, all the instructions I'd learned over the years about bears ran through my head. Don't look them in the eyes. That makes them more aggressive. Immediately I dropped

GRIZZLY

my gaze. What else, what else? My mind felt frozen with fear. My knees were shaking, and I couldn't think. What else? Stop, drop, and roll? No, that was fire. Think. Think!

Oh, yes. Talk to it softly. Let it know you are not a threat. And slowly back away. There was something else about pepper spray, but since I never carried it, that was no good. Keeping my voice soft, I said: "Well, hello there, nice bear. What a nice fishing spot you've found. I'll just leave you to it."

I started backing away as slowly as I could, talking to the ground in front of the bear and sneaking glances at it to see if this was working. The bear growled. Not good. Not a friendly sound. It took a step forward. I had to force myself not to run. They could run really fast, right? I'd read somewhere they could reach speeds of 40 miles per hour. So not good.

That's when the bushes beside me rattled, and baby bear came romping out right beside me. That was bad. Very, very bad. Now I knew why Mama was growling at me. That growl became a roar, and I dropped onto my face, folding my hands protectively behind my neck. My knapsack lay heavy across my back, protecting it. I could hear the bear running toward me, closer and closer. I tensed myself, body shaking and sweating with fear, bracing for the first tearing bite.

Suddenly, a bright light blazed out right above my head. I heard baby bear give a funny yelp of fear, and Mama bear—so close I could smell the stink of her breath—was so startled she reared, overbalanced, and somersaulted backward. I sneaked a glance upward and saw a blazing white figure, almost as tall as a tree, lunge toward the bear with a truly horrible cry. Mama and baby scrambled desperately away from the glowing figure. Baby crashed into the underbrush on the far side of the clearing, and

Mama reared on her hind legs protectively, defying the glowing figure to protect her baby. The blazing figure gave another loud shout, and Mama bear whirled suddenly and raced into the underbrush after her little one. There was the sound of crashing in the underbrush as the grizzlies retreated. Then silence.

I risked another look at the glowing figure and for a moment stared into a familiar pair of eyes. Then the figure vanished, and I was alone in the clearing by the river. I lay prone for a few more minutes to give Mama bear time to get her baby away. Then I slowly rolled over and sat with my head between my knees until the dizziness passed.

As soon as I could walk, I bolted for the truck and locked myself into the warmth and safety of the cab. I lay back in the driver's seat, trembling and too numb to think. My new pole lay in the clearing by the river, but there was no way I was going back to retrieve it. I turned on the car and drove home slowly and carefully, as if I were a student driver taking a first lesson.

Cheryl came hurrying out to the truck when I pulled into the driveway, wondering why I was home so early. I practically fell out of the driver's seat and grabbed her into my arms, shaking all over again with fear and shock. Then I blurted out my story. Cheryl gasped and hugged me as hard as she could when I told her how the bear had attacked me. Then she reared back in astonishment when I told her about the glowing figure that had appeared out of the blue and frightened the bear away.

"Are you telling me you were rescued by an angel?" she said, her eyes huge and a little skeptical.

I laughed shakily. "Not sure if you'd call him an angel," I said. "I think it was Grandpa Dennis who came to the rescue."

Cheryl's mouth drop opened. "Grandpa Dennis?"

"Grandpa Dennis," I confirmed. "Right down to the plaid shirt he always wore when we went fly-fishing together."

"Are you sure—" she began, and saw the look on my face. "You're sure," she said, making it a statement this time. "It sounds crazy, but I can see you're telling the truth." She gave me another big hug. "Well, thank God for Grandpa Dennis. I guess there really are guardian angels after all."

I nodded in agreement, too choked up to speak.

"Next time, you'll listen when I tell you there are grizzly reports going around," she added, drawing me toward the house.

"Yes dear," I said, meaning it. "And I'm going to buy some of that bear pepper spray they've got in the store."

"Several cans of it," Cheryl agreed. "After all, Grandpa Dennis is very busy enjoying himself in heaven. It's not fair to keep pulling him back to earth just to get you out of scrapes!"

I chuckled at her sally—a little feebly, I admit, but it made me feel better to laugh. Deep inside, I felt a small, warm glow at the thought. It was nice to know that Grandpa Dennis was looking out for me from beyond the grave. I gave Cheryl another hug and followed her into the house, thankful to God—and Grandpa Dennis—that I was alive and whole and well. And who knows? Maybe tomorrow I'd go back to the river and see if I could find my new fly rod. With—of course—a huge can of pepper spray!

23

Monster

FLATHEAD LAKE

I was startled out of my half-doze when a big wave suddenly rocked the boat from side to side. I blinked, turning my gaze from the fishing pole to the lake around me. Where had the wave come from? There were no other boats in the vicinity. I'd been drifting down the lake in my little fishing boat all morning, and nothing had passed me for more than an hour. And there was no wind to speak of.

My eyes scanned the water, the beautiful fall foliage adorning the hills and mountains around the lake, the nearby shoreline. There was nothing I saw that could have caused the wave, though I could still see the swell as it broke against the shore. Strange.

I sighed and went back to my peaceful contemplation of rod and reel. It was one of those gorgeous autumn days that are nearly as warm as summer and have the bonus of a colorful leaf display. That morning, I'd happily put my boat into the water and gone fishing. One of the benefits of retirement. You can fish whenever you wish.

I always fish Flathead Lake with my heaviest tackle. I mostly go for the little stuff, catfish and whatnot. But there are sturgeon in this lake, and if one of them hits, it'll break right through the wimpy stuff in no time flat. Some of the white sturgeon grow to 20 feet in length—so they say—and weigh over 1,800 pounds. That's a mighty big fish!

Of course, this being Flathead Lake, you could potentially hook Nessie herself. Yep, the lake was rumored to have a monster. A humdinger of a monster, too. Folks weren't sure if it was one of those super-giant, ancient sturgeons weighing a couple of tons or a real plesiosaur Nessie with a long, undulating body and a prehistoric head. Either way, hooking into the Montana Nessie would definitely mess up your tackle!

I chuckled to myself at the thought. Maybe it was Nessie who'd caused that strange wave.

Just then, the tip of my pole twitched. It was what I'd been waiting for all morning. I set the hook and *whammo,* my pole bent right over until the tip was touching the water! Good lord! Either I'd hooked a whale or some nemesis of the deep had just carried my line under a drowned log. Whales being in short supply in Montana, I figured my hook was stuck in a log. The line was a dead weight, pulling straight down like an anchor. My boat stopped drifting and starting moving back toward the straining line. And then suddenly, the line started ripping off my reel so fast it burned my fingers. I yelped and loosened the brake. There was a fish on my line all right, and jiminy, but it was big!

I let out a whoop and braked the line as gently as I could, trying to slow the critter's progress. It had to be a sturgeon. Nothing else would be ripping line off my pole a hundred feet at a time. There wasn't going to be anything left if it didn't stop running soon. In fact, the tug on the line was so hard and fast, the boat was drifting backwards after it! And gaining speed too! I'd never experienced anything like it.

I was on my feet now, balancing carefully against the moving boat. So heavy and hard was the pull of the fish that water started slapping in over the gunnels and wet my boots. What a fish! Man!

It was moments like this that I regretted fishing alone. If I'd had a buddy along, he could have run the motor and chased the monster fish in the boat, which would have helped me regain some of the line I was losing. I braked a little harder on the line, which was in fairly short supply by now. *Come on, come on! Give a little.* I wasn't about to lose this monster if I could help it. Had to be more than two hundred pounds, the way it was pulling the boat. Jiminy! Maybe I'd hooked one of those eight-hundred pound, twelve-foot sturgeons like they sometimes catch up in British Columbia. Wouldn't that be a fish story! I'd have to drag it ashore. I didn't have a gaff big enough to pull a fish like that in the boat.

At the moment though, it seemed more likely that the fish was going to pull *me* out of the boat. My little fishing craft had picked up quite a bit of speed, and the rear of the boat was dipping so low that I was taking on water. A couple of inches now sloshed around my feet. And my line was almost gone. Suddenly, the sturgeon dove, going deeper and deeper into the lake, bending my pole in two. I bent with it until I could see my reflection in the water. The boat slopped unsteadily side to side for a moment, then stabilized. Then I felt it coming up. And up. And up! Holy cow, it was gonna jump! I was going to see the monster I'd hooked, even if I never brought it into the boat.

MONSTER

Twenty, thirty yards off the stern, a huge head emerged from the water, going up and up. Time seemed to slow as I stared at that huge, prehistoric face. The fish kept rising. And rising. Five feet. Eight feet. Ten feet. Still no sign of a tail. Twelve feet. Fifteen feet. Still no tail visible. And good lord, it was wide. Had to be five-feet wide at the very least. Maybe more. The huge monster shook itself as it rose still higher out of the lake, breaking my line. The release was so sudden that I fell backward into the boat. So I never did see the tail—if it had one. There came a thunderous splash as the creature crashed back into the water, and a moment later the whole boat tipped wildly in the wake of its fall.

I jumped up and scrambled to the side, soaking wet from all the water on the bottom of the boat, and stared as a mammoth brown object streaked away on the surface of the lake. It was going so fast it caused a large wake like the one that I'd felt before. Was that a huge fin on its back? Or was it a coil of body undulating like a snake? I couldn't tell at that distance. I just knew that I'd seen the thing rise almost twenty feet in the air before it crashed down into the lake. Then it dove underwater, and I lost sight of it.

Whew-ee. I fell back against the seat and stared up at the endless blue sky. I'd hooked a monster, all right. And had nothing to show for it but a broken line, a burn on my thumb from braking too hard, and some sopping-wet clothes. But I didn't care! I'd challenge any fisherman on the whole lake to top the fish story I had to tell when I got home! With a huge grin, I sat up, reeled in my broken line—which took ages—and then turned on the motor and headed toward home.

Sacred Place

PRYOR MOUNTAINS

It was a fine day in late summer. The sun was sparkling, the sky was blue, and I felt like hunting. So did the dogs. So we went. I got three of the very best German shorthaired pointers in Montana, and they were bouncing around like puppies in their excitement. I whistled them to order, and we headed for the mountains, taking one of our favorite hiking trails.

We passed right by old Abe's gate on our way into the back country, and he gave us a grin and a hello. "Hey, Bart, got something here for you!" he called. I swerved and went over to the fence. Abe held out a big white handkerchief. I recognized it as the one I'd used to patch up his arm when he got cut so bad out fishing. "My missus washed it up real good, and I've been carrying it in my pocket the last few days, hoping you'd wander by. When we going fishing again?"

"I'm hunting today. How about next weekend if the weather stays nice?"

We set a day and time, and Abe spent a few more minutes making a fuss over the dogs, especially Lady, who was a particular friend of his. Then I waved goodbye and we were off into the rugged beauty of the mountains, looking for mule deer or whatever game happened across my path that day. Frankly, I didn't care if I saw anything at all. Just being outside was enough.

"Maybe we'll see some of the wild horses," I said cheerfully to Lady. She wagged her short, cropped tail delightedly and then raced up to join Deuce and Domino. We ranged far and wide that morning, making a large circle through the rolling native grasslands, pines, and steep canyons that made up the eastern slope of the Pryor Mountains. I spotted some mule deer just out of gunshot range. Then Lady and Domino went on point, and I flushed and shot a couple of partridges. They'd make a good supper for us all.

I glanced down at Deuce, who took that opportunity to sit down, raise his hind leg, and scratch indecorously. "Some bird dog you turned out to be," I said jokingly. He blinked at me and then jumped up and ran after the others. He was the youngest of my three and still learning the finer points of hunting.

By midafternoon, we'd completed two-thirds of our circuit. I'd tried to time it so we'd be back at home before dark, but I'd ranged a bit further afield than I'd planned, and we'd have to hustle a bit now. As we headed eastward, I spotted a low, rugged canyon that I'd never noticed before. It was hard to see unless you were at precisely the right angle on the hillside. Inside the canyon, I glimpsed some interesting rock formations. I whistled for the dogs and headed into the canyon. Just a quick look now, I promised myself, and then we would head home.

The walls of the canyon were steep, and already it lay in shadow. Something about it was off-putting. It felt as if someone were watching me as I picked my way carefully down toward the formations I'd seen from the top. The dogs were at my heels, and they'd stop every once in a while and sniff the air nervously. I wasn't sure I liked this canyon, now that I was in it, but since I was already halfway down, I kept going.

A bit of color caught my eye, and I took a closer look at the walls of the canyon. There were drawings on them of strange little men that resembled pygmy sasquatches with sharp teeth. The sight of them made my skin crawl. The dogs were crowded so close to me now that Lady knocked into my legs. Maybe that's what made me lose balance. All I really remember was slipping suddenly on loose gravel and rolling down the steep slope, my rifle clutched to my side.

My fall was stopped abruptly when I hit a shelf of rock about ten feet below, and my leg twisted painfully under me. I heard something crack and was in sudden agony. I yelped and clutched at my leg, ignoring a puff of cool air that chilled my back. I moaned in agony as the dogs came leaping down to surround me, barking shrilly. Lady nosed me worriedly, and I had to make them sit before their milling about hurt my already-throbbing leg any further.

When the first agony of my injury had abated, I forced myself to take note of my surroundings. I lay at the entrance to a cave, the walls of which were covered with pictographs of those same twisted creatures. I remembered hearing from a Crow friend of mine that dwarfs inhabited these mountains, but I'd put that down as an old legend. But the pictures around me were pretty graphic, showing little wild men hunting bighorn sheep and elk and other creatures with their stone knives and eating their flesh with relish. They had sharp teeth that would have looked good on a vampire. I was sweating with pain, and my leg had already swollen so much my jeans felt tight. But my skin grew cold, and goose bumps formed all over my arms as I stared at the pictures and tried to think about what to do. My leg seemed to be broken, and there was no way I could walk out of here. My wife was away for the weekend and wouldn't even miss me until she got home late Sunday night. The only one who knew I was out hunting today was Abe.

Remembering the handkerchief he'd given me, I pulled it out and fumbled in my other pocket until I found the pen I always carried. On the handkerchief, I shakily wrote: "Broken leg. Need Help. Bart." I jotted a few rough directions to the canyon below the message and then thrust the handkerchief at Lady to smell, hoping she'd get Abe's scent. Tying the handkerchief to her collar, I said: "Lady, go fetch Abe. Go get Abe and bring him here. Go get Abe." She stared at me with solemn eyes. Her short tail twitched. Then she was off and away up the canyon. I followed her with my eyes, hoping she'd understood me.

Lady was out of sight when I felt a sudden, sharp gust of air and heard a thud, as if someone had shot an arrow. Lady gave a sudden yelp of pain, and I heard her scrabbling for balance before she continued running out of the mouth of the canyon. My whole body went rigid. Had someone just shot my dog? How could that be? We were alone in the canyon. Weren't we?

I shuddered, remembering the pictures on the walls of the cave behind me. I was feeling lightheaded with pain and fear, but caution made me look around for my rifle. It had landed a few yards away, by the outer wall of the cave. I crawled toward it slowly, inch by slow inch. It hurt my leg terribly and worried the dogs, but I kept going. I wanted solid rock at my back and a rifle in my hand. In my current condition, I needed some protection in case a bear or a bobcat or some other predator happened along. Deuce and Domino stayed with me, nuzzling me and licking my face and whimpering in sympathy.

When I was finally in place, with the rock firmly at my back and my rifle on my lap, I felt better, though my head was swimming. The dogs took up spots on either side of me and kept watch as I slid in and out of consciousness. Their noses kept twitching as if they smelled something they didn't like.

In my lucid moments, I tried to calculate how long it would take Lady to get to Abe. We'd been making a big circle during our hunt, and we were probably forty-five minutes from Abe's place by now. So ninety minutes to and from, plus however long it took Lady to find Abe and make him understand what was needed. Two hours at least. Maybe more. That was too darn close to sundown for my comfort. I didn't want to lie out here all night in a creepy canyon with a broken leg. Especially not now. In my current position, I could make out a few of those rock formations I'd been coming down the canyon to see. From this angle, they looked like rough-hewn statues of little man dancing triumphantly around a large dead creature of some kind. I shuddered. One of the paintings on the wall opposite me depicted dwarf-like creatures eating the bloody hearts of their kill in some strange sort of sacred ritual. I shuddered and lost consciousness again.

When I woke, sunlight had completely gone from the canyon, and the dogs were growling. I looked out through the twilight and saw two—no, four—small figures watching me from the deepening shadows under the stony tableau. It looked like they were holding bows. As I watched, one of them knocked an arrow and pointed it at me. Or was it at the dogs?

Deuce barked suddenly and charged toward the small creatures. I called him back, holding tightly to Domino's collar. Domino was on his feet and growling menacingly at the little figures.

I yelled again for Deuce, but he kept on running as if he hadn't heard me. Suddenly, the air was full of arrows, and Deuce went down. Half a dozen small figures in rough animal skins ran toward my fallen dog, and I saw a stone knife rise up, fall. Deuce gave a coughing sort of yelp that died away quickly.

Suddenly, I was furious. I half rose, grunting with the agony of movement, and fell back against the stone wall of the canyon. "That was my dog!" I shouted, raising my gun. "Leave him alone!" I fumbled as I turned off the safety, took aim at the stone tableau over the capering figures and fired a shot. The little figures froze and then whirled to look at me. "Leave him alone!" I shouted again. In the dim light, I could see blood staining the mouth of one of the figures—the one wearing a fancy sort of cap stuck with eagle feathers. Domino crouched beside me, still growling faintly, but obeying my command to stay.

"You have invaded our sacred place against our sacred laws," the dwarf with the bloody mouth said in curiously accented English. "Be glad we have just taken your dog."

As quickly as they had appeared, the dwarfs were gone, carrying the body of Deuce away with them. I would have thought the whole thing a bad dream if it hadn't been for the blood-stained spot before me.

A moment later, I heard Abe's voice calling down from the top of the canyon. "Bart, are you there? I heard a gunshot." Bright searchlights appeared, illuminating the twilight, and Lady rushed up to me as Abe came down the canyon with a mountain rescue team. As they loaded me onto a stretcher, Abe

SACRED PLACE

asked me if I wanted him to find Deuce. I shook my head. "I think a bear got him," I said, not wanting to talk about the strange little men I had seen or to draw anyone else's attention to their sacred place. Better to let dead dogs lie.

The rescue team carried me out of the canyon and loaded me into their vehicle. Abe and the two dogs crowded in behind, and we rode away from the canyon into the twilight of a late-summer night. Behind us, the last of the pink and orange clouds turned dark purple, then gray, then midnight blue.

I made a vow, then and there, that I would never return to the sacred canyon. But perhaps I would tell my Crow friend the true story about my accident. I think he would like to hear about the dwarfs.

25

The Stone

SHELBY

The young man grew up in the shadow of the stone, listening to the elders and watching the medicine man in his tribe use the stone to predict the future. The stone was a sacred place—a huge wall covered with pictures that mysteriously appeared and disappeared. The elders said that the pictures were drawn by the hand of the spirits to help guide the people in the true way. All the holy men in the region came to consult the stone, seeking to discover what the future held for their people. Would there be a hard winter? Many buffalo herds or few? Who would live and who would die in the season to come? The young man was fascinated by the stone. And he knew one day he would be one of those holy men who read the pictures on the stone, who understood what they meant.

In time, the young man started working with his tribe's medicine man and learning the sacred secrets and holy chants. Finally, he was taken to the stone. At first, the pictures were a jumble in his mind. They made no sense. How could these pictures tell the future? But when he stilled his mind, when he opened his senses, the meaning came. He saw the pictures one at a time in his mind, as if a light fell upon them. The seeming

THE STONE

randomness vanished, and a new order imposed itself. He saw a deer, a tree, a cougar, a man's face. Combined, the pictures told of an unexpected death while out hunting. And it was so. The injured warrior was found and carried home. He had been mauled almost beyond recognition by a cougar that had attacked him while he was hunting deer. He died the next day.

Slowly, it grew easier for the young man to read the stone. He would pose a question, still his mind, and then watch the symbols to see which ones swam to the front of his "seer vision." In this way, he was able to tell his people of a shift in the buffalo herds a week before the older medicine man saw it. And the young man led the warriors in a very successful buffalo jump, with many beasts killed and dressed for the hard winter he foresaw for them.

The old medicine man was proud of his student and gave way gracefully as the talented young man proved the better seer. And yet, being a seer was not all the medicine man had to teach the young man, if he had been willing to listen. But he was not. He grew proud of his seer's skill, proud of the way all the maidens of the tribe vied for his attention. And in his pride, he valued himself above all others, until he felt that he deserved anything he desired.

And he desired what he could not have. The wife of Swift Runner, the bravest of the tribes' warriors, caught his eye. She was fair as the summer sky, soft-spoken as the gentlest breeze, and as sweet of manner as honey on the tongue. The young medicine man wanted her. And to gain her, he turned his mind away from his sacred seer's vision. In his heart, he plotted murder. The stone would sometimes show the face of a warrior doomed to die in that season, as it had once shown him the man who was mauled by a cougar. So the young medicine man searched the stone each day for the face of Swift Runner. When it did not appear, he crept out to the stone in the night and himself drew the face of the warrior among the sacred drawings.

Two days later, he brought the old medicine man with him to visit the stone, telling his elder—with much lamentation— that he had foreseen the death of a member of their tribe. When they arrived after fasting and praying for several hours, the young medicine man brought the old one's attention to the new face that had appeared among the symbols. The old man was troubled when he saw it. Yes, it was clearly there on the stone. Yes, it was Swift Runner. But somehow, the picture did not ring true in his mind. He rejected the sign instantly as false, though he could not say how he knew this. He said nothing of his suspicions to the young medicine man. Instead, he listened to the young man's interpretation of the future, which included the death of Swift Runner, observing his face closely during the telling. Then he sat himself down and conducted his own vision quest upon the stone.

One after another, the symbols appeared to the old man. Many buffalo. A baby boy, followed by the face of the chief. A couple entwined by a love knot. A twisted tongue. A hand holding a bloody knife. A dying warrior. The old man's sight cleared at last, and he gazed upon the too-eager face of the young medicine man. The old man had foreseen the coming of many buffalo, a new marriage in the tribe, the birth of a son to the chief, and the betrayal of a warrior by a man with a lying tongue. His wise old eyes had seen many things through the years, and what he saw now in the face of the young medicine man worried him. He had not missed the way the young man looked at Swift Runner's wife.

The old man placated the young medicine man with a few words about a dying warrior, using his skill with language to hint that the young medicine man might be correct in his interpretation without actually agreeing with him. It took all his training to keep his face from betraying his true thoughts.

When he returned to the village, the old medicine man went privately and spoke to the chief of his suspicions. So a trap was laid for the young medicine man. The chief called his counselors together and asked the young medicine man to tell them what the near future held for the tribe. With sad countenance, he spoke of an upcoming skirmish between their warriors and a band from a rival tribe that would result in death. The men must be warned—particularly Swift Runner—for whom he foresaw great danger. Accordingly, the message went out among the warriors to watch carefully for an attack by the enemy, and for Swift Runner in particular to take great care.

But the chief secretly set several men to watch the young medicine man and report back on anything suspicious they observed. And so it was that they followed the young man the next evening to a secret glen, where he met with representatives from a neighboring tribe and paid them with several horses and other bribes to attack the warriors the next time they rode out to hunt—and to kill Swift Runner.

The witnesses reported back to the chief as soon as the young medicine man returned to his lodge. Immediately, the chief and the old medicine man summoned the young man to them. "Walk with us," they said. "We would hear more of this rival tribe who threatens us." The young medicine man was flattered by their interest. As the three men walked slowly along the path leading to the stone, he spun a detailed lie about the vision he had seen concerning Swift Runner. So true did it become in his mind that when he saw Swift Runner waiting for them beside the stone, he felt it was all a-piece with the tale of treachery he had just spun for his chief.

"But it is not I who have been betrayed by our neighbors," the warrior said as the three men approached the sacred stone. "It is you who have betrayed your people with your lies."

And so saying, Swift Runner drew a knife from his belt. The two older men stepped away from the young medicine man, who knew then that he must fight Swift Runner to the death. His face twisted in anger as he pulled out his own knife and tensed his body for the confrontation.

At that moment, the picture of Swift Runner on the stone began to glow with a red-hot light that throbbed eerily and made the air sizzle with electricity. The picture grew in size until it dominated the face of the stone, and a huge, swirling, dark funnel appeared at the center. The funnel seemed to extend deep into unknown dimensions, and a wild wind sprang out of it, filled with the smells of death and blood and decay. All four men sprang backward from the stone, filled with terrible fear. But the red light whipped suddenly forward like lightning, and tendrils of wind mixed with light wrapped around the young medicine man's limbs. He struggled in panic but was yanked swiftly toward the mouth of the funnel. With a scream that ever-after haunted the nightmares of the watching tribesmen, the young medicine man fell into the yawning mouth of the funnel. It snapped shut like the mouth of a hungry monster. The red light and howling wind died away, and the sacred stone was still and silent once more. The picture of Swift Runner had vanished with the young medicine man who had drawn it.

Shaken, Swift Runner, the chief, and the old medicine man left the sacred stone and returned to the village. The people were summoned, and the betrayal and subsequent death of the young medicine man were reported to them. Messengers were sent to the neighboring tribe to relay the story to them as well, and the men who had conspired with the young medicine man were disciplined severely.

And so the old medicine man resumed his role as the village seer, and from that day onward, no one ever again tried to use the stone for personal gain. Clearly, the spirits were watching.

26

Bloody Mary Returns

BOZEMAN

My stepmother was vile. I guess most kids think that when their father remarries. But in this case, it was true. The woman only married Father because he was rich. And she *hated* children. There were three of us—me (Marie), my middle brother Richard, and my youngest brother Charles. We were the price stepmother Gerta paid for being rich. And we were all that stood between her and inheriting Father's money when he died. So she took steps against us.

She sent Charles away to boarding school overseas. The school had a scholarly reputation, but it was also known to be full of bullies and run with strict discipline. Not a place where a delicate child like Charles, who had been sickly as a baby, would thrive. He was miserable there. Yet somehow Gerta contrived to keep him there for all but the summer holidays, and when he came home the first year he was pale and thin with dark circles under his eyes that looked like bruises. He cried—he actually cried!—when Father told him he had to go back to the school. But Father didn't listen to him. Gerta thought it would be good for Charles to go there, and so Charles went.

I did everything I could—writing encouraging letters and

making daily phone calls—until Gerta said the calls were too expensive and restricted them to five minutes once a month. I even got Father to book me a ticket to Europe so I could visit Charles. Gerta was enraged when she found out. Her blue eyes went so cold it made chills run up my spine, and her pink mouth thinned into a bitter line that bade ill for me since I had dared to interfere. Two days before my plane left for Europe, the school called and told us that Charles had climbed up to the tallest tower and flung himself off. He was dead.

Father was shocked, of course, and Gerta quietly triumphant. For a few months, Father paid more attention to Richard and me then he had since our mother died. But Gerta was beautiful and had a winning manner that soon drew Father's attention away from us. And now that one of her hated stepchildren was dead, Gerta focused on another. Poor Richard was next.

Richard was a sturdy chap who was about to enter high school, and sports were his passion. He would have thrived at the boarding school that had killed Charles. So Gerta sent him to an arts school instead. He hated it, but Gerta told Father he had "talent," so there he went. (You'd think my Father would have learned his lesson with Charles!)

Richard was a survivor, so he grimly practiced piano and violin when he would rather have played soccer and football. But Gerta was clever. She introduced Richard to a couple of high school boys who were everything Richard wanted to be—rich, popular, on the football team. And heavy users of drugs. Gerta made sure Richard had a very large allowance, and she kept increasing it as Richard was drawn deeper and deeper under the influence. Until one day Richard overdosed, and Gerta had only one stepchild left. Me.

I was sure (sure!) that Gerta knew Richard was taking drugs in his room that day. She knew he was ill and possibly dying in there. If she'd "found" him even ten minutes sooner, his life would have been saved. So said the doctor, and I believed him. But Father wouldn't believe me. He was angry whenever I said anything against Gerta and told me to hold my tongue. Still, I knew I was next, and I was sure that Father would not live long after willing his fortune over to his wife. I decided that if Gerta got too bad, I would run away and live secretly with my aunt in Missoula until I turned eighteen.

From the moment Richard's body was found in his room, I forced myself to be a model child. My homework was always done on time. I was polite to Gerta and her friends. I even went on all the family excursions with Gerta and Father—even the dangerous ones like shark-fishing. (You can be sure that I took care to be "seasick" and stayed indoors and away from the edge of the boat on that particular outing!) But Gerta was clever. On a family vacation to New York City, everyone thought it was an accident when I fell onto the subway in front of an oncoming train. I managed to roll out of the way in time, but the escape was way too close for comfort.

After that trip, I decided the only way to be safe was to run away. But before I could make my getaway, my father brought me the sad news that my aunt in Missoula had died suddenly in her sleep, poisoned by person or persons unknown. I was appalled. How had Gerta known? But she had—I could tell from the smirk on her face.

I went to my room that night and locked myself in to think. I could run away, but the small amount of money I had wouldn't last long. And I'd need to finish high school or my chances of getting a good job were nil. Besides, Gerta would still be out there somewhere. If she could hire someone to poison my only living relative (besides Father), she could hire someone to kill me, whether I was living at home or not.

There was only one thing I could think of. And it was a terrible thing. A secret passed down in my mother's family for many generations. Before my great-grandfather had come to Montana as a gold prospector, he had lived in an old-time German community in Pennsylvania where the villagers still lived in fear of a curse placed upon them long ago by a witch named Bloody Mary.

The story, as it was told to my mother and later to me, went something like this. Bloody Mary lived deep in the forest in a tiny cottage and sold herbal remedies for a living. Folks living in the town nearby said she was a witch, and none dared cross the old crone for fear that their cows would go dry, their food-stores rot away before winter, their children take sick of fever, or any number of terrible things that an angry witch could do to her neighbors.

Then the little girls in the village began to disappear, one by one. No one could find out where they had gone. Grief-stricken families searched the woods, the local buildings, and all the houses and barns, but there was no sign of the missing girls. A few brave souls even went to Bloody Mary's home in the woods to see if the witch had taken the girls, but she denied any knowledge of the disappearances. Still, it was noted that her haggard appearance had changed. She looked younger, more attractive. The neighbors were suspicious, but they could find no proof that the witch had taken their young ones.

Then came the night when the daughter of the blacksmith

rose from her bed and walked outside, following an enchanted sound no one else could hear. The blacksmith's wife had a toothache and was sitting up in the kitchen treating the tooth with an herbal remedy when her daughter left the house. She screamed for her husband and followed the girl out the door. The blacksmith came running in his nightshirt. Together, they tried to restrain the girl, but she kept breaking away from them and heading out of town.

The desperate cries of the blacksmith and his wife woke the neighbors. They came to assist the frantic couple. Suddenly, a sharp-eyed farmer gave a shout and pointed toward a strange light at the edge of the woods. A few townsmen followed him out into the field and saw Bloody Mary standing beside a large oak tree, holding a magic mirror that was pointed toward the blacksmith's house. She was glowing with an unearthly light as she set her evil spell upon the blacksmith's daughter.

The townsmen grabbed their guns and their pitchforks and ran toward the witch. When she heard the commotion, Bloody Mary broke off her spell and fled back into the woods. The far-sighted farmer had loaded his gun with silver bullets in case the witch ever came after his daughter. Now he took aim and shot at her. The bullet hit Bloody Mary in the hip and she fell to the ground. The angry townsmen leapt upon her and carried her back into the field, where they built a huge bonfire and burned her at the stake. As she burned, Bloody Mary screamed a curse at the villagers. If any of the villagers—or any of their descendents—ever mentioned her name aloud before a mirror, she would send her spirit to revenge herself upon them for her terrible death.

When she was dead, the villagers went to the house in the

wood and found the unmarked graves of the little girls the evil witch had murdered. She had used their blood to make herself young again.

According to my great-grandfather, the curse laid on the families descended from those villagers was very real. One young man, born a few years after the witch's death at the stake, decided the story was a lot of nonsense. When he was fourteen, he foolishly chanted Bloody Mary's name three times before a darkened mirror. Immediately, the vengeful spirit of the witch appeared and tore him to pieces, ripping his soul right out of his mutilated body and carrying it back into the mirror with her to burn in torment as Bloody Mary had once burned. To this day, the young man's spirit was still trapped with Bloody Mary in the mirror.

Of course, the true story had gotten mixed up over the years, as it was passed down first in the village and then all over the country. These days, schoolkids everywhere scared themselves silly chanting Bloody Mary's name in front of darkened mirrors during sleepover parties, and nothing happened to them. So no one really believed in the curse. Of course, no one knew the real story of Bloody Mary. That was a deep secret handed down by the villagers of long ago. But I was a direct descendant of the townsfolk, and I knew how to summon the witch. You had to use a mirror owned by someone in the direct bloodline of one of the original families that lived in Bloody Mary's village. And the witch's name must be spoken by candlelight a certain number of times in the villagers' native German.

It was an evil thing to do, I knew. But it seemed the only way to save my life. It was either Gerta or me. If I didn't fight back, I was dead. So I took my hard-earned money and went out to a specialty store to buy hand-dipped, beeswax candles. Black ones. I followed my mother's directions carefully, placing them at certain intervals around the living room so that they reflected in the huge mirror behind the couch. Then I lit each one, speaking the spell passed down in my mother's family. And I waited. Father was away on a business trip, and Gerta was out at a party with her latest boyfriend. She came home late and scolded me for staying up to study. Her voice was playful and light—I hated that voice. It made her sound like she was nice. But there was a note of suspicion underlying her words, and she stared hard at the flickering black candles.

"Holding a séance, little Marie?" she asked, emphasizing the word *little*, knowing I hated it when she called me that.

"I just like working by candlelight," I said mendaciously, turning a page in my textbook.

Gerta frowned. "You know, little Marie, I think it's time we had a talk," she said, walking over to the large mirror behind the couch and fluffing up her golden hair.

"Yes," I said softly. "We should. You killed my brothers. And my aunt. But I won't let you kill me."

Gerta laughed. "As if you stood a chance against me!" she said, tossing her long blond hair up behind her shoulders.

That was when I spoke the name of Bloody Mary in the native tongue of my ancestors. Once. Twice. Three times. Inside the mirror, the image of Gerta burst into flames, and another face looked out. It was the malevolent face of a twisted old crone, ruined with age, and altogether evil. I ducked behind the chair as Gerta gave a scream of sheer terror, her eyes fixed on the witch in the mirror.

As I watched from my hiding place, heat burst forth from

BLOODY MARY RETURNS

the mirror, blistering Gerta's beautiful alabaster skin. Around the room, the black candles blazed up tall and bright and then went out. I could hear flames roaring as the witch laughed evilly and held out her arms toward my stepmother. "Gerta," crooned Bloody Mary. "Come to me, Gerta." And she took my stepmother into her arms.

Gerta's terrified scream was suddenly cut off. The flames disappeared as rapidly as they had come. When I peeked out from behind the couch, Gerta and Bloody Mary were gone, and the mirror was calmly reflecting the darkened living room. It was over. I had won.

I called Father at his hotel the next morning to tell him that Gerta hadn't slept at home. (Well, it was true!) He wasn't pleased. He called a few of her friends from his hotel room and quickly discovered she had been carrying on with another man. With several, if the truth be known. Father hated infidelity. He flew home at once to confront Gerta, but she was still missing; presumably she had run away with one of her flames.

Somehow, Father managed to divorce Gerta without ever trying to find her. And since she had no family in the area except us, no one ever questioned the story of her runaway elopement, and no one ever tried to locate her. Gerta was gone for good. And Father and I were safe at last.

27

Snow Bird

GLACIER NATIONAL PARK

The storm came howling down out of the mountains so fast and furious that Snow Bird barely made it back to her lodge on the far side of the village before a fog of icy crystals whipped around her, obscuring everything from sight. It was an unexpected blizzard in early autumn, and it took everyone in the village completely by surprise.

She was shaking with cold when she entered the lodge and found her young bridegroom piling wood up against one wall. They were newly wed, and the sight of her husband made Snow Bird's heart beat faster and her breath catch in her chest. His dark hair was glossy and long, his eyes the deepest black, and he stood tall with broad shoulders and a slim waist. In contrast, Snow Bird was small and quick and lively with dark hair that had a tendency to curl on humid days and eyes that were an unusual golden-brown with glints of green in their depths. Bearclaw was considered the bravest of the warriors in their village, and Snow Bird was already known as a wise woman for the visions sent to her by the spirits and for her cunning with herbs.

Already, the chill was seeping into the lodge, and Bearclaw tossed his bride a blanket before building up the fire. Snow Bird pulled it across her shoulders thankfully as the demon voices of the blizzard howled and wept and shrieked around the lodge. There was an inhuman note to the voices in the wind that sent a shudder up her spine. She found something almost menacing about the unexpected storm, so early in the season. For a moment, a shape flickered at the edge of her vision. Snow Bird blinked, trying to bring it into focus as the medicine man had instructed her long ago, when he learned of her gift. But it was gone. She shrugged and went to gather the bedding and bring it to warm by the fire.

They spent the next two days huddled over the fire as the storm raged outside. Once, Bearclaw had gone outside to gather more wood and had almost gotten lost, though the pile stood right beside the door. The storm was so fierce that it had blown him off his feet twice before he got enough wood into the lodge to last them through the night. Snow Bird fretted as she dried off the wood and fed the small pieces to the flames.

"Smiling Cloud is ill," she said to her husband. "She needs more of my herbal medicine. I must go to her."

Bearclaw shook his head. "You cannot. We are only a few yards from the next lodge, but it is invisible to me in the storm. To go out in the blizzard now will surely cause your death!"

Snow Bird nodded reluctantly, unable to shake the feeling growing inside her that Smiling Cloud needed help. The feeling of menace that had come to her at the beginning of the storm returned, and the howling voices in the wind made her neck and scalp prickle. She shuddered, and Bearclaw put his arm around her, thinking she was cold. They huddled together under the blankets, practically sitting on top of the fire to stay warm, and told each other stories to pass the time. But still, Snow Bird was nervous, uneasy. Something was wrong. The very air of the lodge seemed dark with the wrongness. Her nerves stretched tight until she was ready to shriek at the wrongness to go away. But still the storm raged on, hour after dark hour.

Snow Bird woke suddenly in the night, screaming in terror, her voice mixing with the howls and shrieks of the blizzard around her. Her nostrils were filled with a sickly sweet, rotten stench, and her staring, blank eyes were blinded by visions of tattered buffalo hide, icy white snow, and blood. "What is it? My love, what is wrong?" Bearclaw gasped, taking his shuddering wife by the shoulders and shaking her, willing her eyes to focus on his face instead of the visions that terrified her. But Snow Bird was still lost in her dreams. Face crumpled with fear, eyes burning with a glint of silver in their black depths, she gagged at the stench of sweet decay, animal musk, and blood she still smelled and gasped: "Death. I see death." Her words took on the poetic ring they always had when she was seeing a vision. "Ripping and tearing. Blood and ice. A cold heart. A head— severed!" The last word was a scream, and she fell into his arms, gasping and shaking while he soothed her.

She raised her head at last, and her eyes had lost the silvery tint of vision. "Can you not smell it?" she asked, nose twitching slightly as the smell of sickly sweet decay slowly dissipated from the lodge. Bearclaw shook his head. He had not her gift for visions, and of this he was heartily glad. "I smell nothing," he told his beloved. She nodded sadly, and they cuddled into the blankets again. The fireside was warm, but Snow Bird was as cold as ice in her husband's arms, and it took more than an hour for her shaking to stop and her breathing to grow regular again.

There was silence at dawn. The blizzard was over. Snow Bird woke early with the silence ringing in her ears. She sat up, shaking in dread. Her movement woke Bearclaw, who rose and poked up the fire.

"I must see to Smiling Cloud," Snow Bird said into the dreadful stillness after the storm. Each word fell like a pebble into a quiet pond. They seemed to ripple out into the silence, and each ripple made the shadows a little deeper, the fear a little stronger. She could still smell blood at the back of everything, and with it was a stench like rotting fruit.

"I will come with you," Bearclaw said firmly. They wrapped themselves in their warmest garments and furs, and Bearclaw broke a path through the snow toward the old couple's lodge at the edge of the village. The sun was sparkling on the colored leaves of the trees, weighted down with their burden of snow. The white landscape glittered so much it hurt Snow Bird's eyes. Squinting against the light, her eyes smarting with tears, she did not see at first why Bearclaw stopped so suddenly. Then he said: "Turn around, Snow Bird. Turn around and go back to the lodge. Right now!"

Something in his voice made Snow Bird's skin crawl. She pushed past her stunned husband and stared at the old couple's lodge, lying torn and tattered on its side in the snow. The icy drifts around it were a strange, pinkish color. It took her a moment to recognize a severed hand lying half-buried in a snowdrift with a beaded bracelet around the wrist. The hand belonged to Smiling Cloud.

Snow Bird did not scream. It might have been better if she had. She just stared at the bloody stump in front of her, the vision from the previous night swirling in front of her unseeing eyes. The world pitched and swayed and then went dark. She did not feel herself fall.

It seemed a long time later when her eyes opened to the filtered daylight inside her lodge. Her husband's worried face stared down into hers, his frown smoothing away instantly when he saw her eyes open. Her breath caught in her chest and she ached with love at the sight of his beloved face. For a moment, everything was as perfect as it had been from the day they had wed. And then she remembered Smiling Cloud.

She lunged upward with a soft cry of horror, and Bearclaw caught her close. "They think it was a rogue grizzly," he said softly into her ear. "Caught out in the blizzard and disoriented. Apparently, it killed Smiling Cloud and Two Trees, but we could only find . . . pieces . . . of Smiling Cloud." He gulped at the grisly memory, sweat beading his forehead in spite of the chill seeping through the lodge as the fire burned low. "It seems the grizzly dragged Two Trees' body away."

Snow Bird's eyes clouded with doubt and her nostrils twitched as she remembered the sweetly rotten animal smell around her friends' lodge. That was not the smell of a grizzly. And her vision . . . she shuddered at the thought. *Please let it be a grizzly*, she prayed. *Please.*

The village was in an uproar over the attack. The warriors searched through the glistening, hard-packed snow for any traces of Two Trees or the rogue grizzly. But none were found. Snow Bird and the village medicine man exchanged a glance during the tribal meeting that followed the futile search, and then both looked away uneasily, neither ready to admit what was in both of their minds. It must be a rogue grizzly. It must.

The villagers were instructed to watch out for the rogue grizzly, and children were told to remain within the boundaries of the village until the bear was caught and killed. As a warm autumn breeze swept in from the south and began melting the snow, several hunting parties rode out from the village in differing directions, their faces grim with purpose. They would kill a bear today. But that could never erase the horror of what had happened. The rest of the villagers buried the gnawed and tooth-marked pieces that were all that remained of poor Smiling Cloud. They never did find her head.

Two grizzlies were discovered in the vicinity and killed. There was no rejoicing over the occasion. The meat was distributed among several families and eaten in silence. But the gloom over the village was slowly invaded by the happy whistling of the wind in the grasses, by the whistle of birds who had crept out from their nests and were preparing for the journey south, by the incessant drip-drip of the melting snow. One day passed, then two, and the memory of the freak storm receded with the melting snow. Smiling Cloud and Two Trees were mourned, but life went on. People started to smile again. Children began running through the woods and playing. The women prepared their food stores and lodges for a hard winter, and the men went out to hunt.

Yet Snow Bird could not shake a growing uneasiness, the sense of menace that seemed to stare down at her from the looming mountains. The autumn was lovely, the air crisp and cool. But behind the pleasant façade, something was not quite as it should be. Something lurked, watching the small, isolated village go about its business, waiting for the right moment to strike. She tried to laugh off the prickling of her scalp, the knot in her stomach. But each time she passed the medicine man in the village, he avoided her gaze. She would watch his retreating figure, her heart heavy with fear, knowing he was not avoiding her so much as the knowledge given to her by her visions. He knew—as did she—that it was not a grizzly that had killed Smiling Cloud. It was something much worse. By avoiding one another, they could deny, at least for a time, the suspicion growing in both of them. Perhaps they were wrong.

But they were not. Two weeks after the freak autumn blizzard, a tattered figure stumbled into the village. His head lolled a bit to one side, his arms and shoulders were scratched under his clothing, and he walked as if his feet hurt with every step he took. But he was alive. It took a moment for the villagers to recognize the ragged, pathetic figure as Two Trees. Then they exclaimed and gathered around him, and he was gently carried to the medicine man's lodge to be tended.

Two Trees was feverish at first. He tossed and turned for days, muttering strange things during his illness as the autumn leaves fell from the trees and the small woodland creatures squabbled over nuts and berries, readying themselves for winter. When he recovered his wits, Two Trees could not remember anything of the night Smiling Cloud had died, and he did not want to talk about it. He withdrew deep inside his own head, and he stared hungrily around him with eyes so dark they were almost red. People became uneasy in his presence, for he would lick his lips as they approached and watch their every move like a panther waiting to strike.

No one said a word about it. But parents kept their children away from the medicine man's lodge during Two Trees' convalescence, and the warriors watched him warily. Now Snow

Bird and the medicine man were not the only ones to suspect the truth behind Smiling Cloud's death. Everyone in the tribe was wondering if it really was a grizzly that had killed her and injured Two Trees. Or something darker.

The word was on everyone's mind. Wendigo. But no one said it aloud. No one dared voice the thought. They kept their minds busy with the harvest, with winter preparations. And as the days passed, and Two Trees grew stronger, more like himself, their fear lessened. Perhaps they were wrong.

Then Sings Like A Bird, the chief's six-year-old daughter, disappeared out of the chief's lodge one evening just before supper. Her mother was frantic when she found her missing. Her panic spread quickly among all the women, among the old men. And then everyone caught it, and they turned the village upside down searching for the child. Two Trees searched with the others, his dark eyes gleaming red whenever he passed through the shadows.

It was Snow Bird who found the child's little, half-eaten body dragged under low bushes several hundred yards from camp. Only a bit of moccasin was showing, but her keen eyes spotted it, and she trembled as she approached the underbrush, already knowing what she would see. Suddenly, as silent as a stalking panther, Two Trees was at her side.

"What do you see, little Bird?" he hissed, holding out the sibilant *s* like a snake.

The seer turned to look at the battered man, with his lolling head and red eyes. Faintly, she could smell the stench of rotting fruit and animal musk emanating from his skin as the evil spirit inside him grew stronger. Her own eyes glinted with silver as she said: "I see evil, Two Trees. I see Wendigo." Two Trees hissed at the word and raised his hands toward her throat. But he was knocked over from behind by Bearclaw, who had been searching near his beloved wife, afraid to let her out of his sight with Two Trees wandering in the woods.

The two men rolled over tree roots and thorns, fighting each other viciously, hand to hand. Two Trees had a strength that was inhuman, and even Bearclaw—the mightiest of the warriors in the tribe—was hard pressed to keep the evil Wendigo off his throat. Snow Bird, calling desperately for help, leapt onto the back of the crazed man, pulling his hands away from her husband. Her cry aroused the searchers, and in a moment Two Trees was subdued by several warriors. He was dragged toward the chief's lodge, followed by the grim-faced Bearclaw bearing a very small, bloody burden, half its little body torn away and human tooth marks visible in its tiny throat. The child's mother screamed when she saw her little daughter thus and threw herself upon the Wendigo who had murdered and eaten her child, trying to tear out his eyes. But the others restrained her, and her husband laid a tender hand on her cheek and promised her justice.

Two Trees was babbling insanely now about a huge figure that had loomed out of the snowstorm and called him by name. He spoke of the evil Wendigo spirit that had dragged him high above the clouds, running with him before the storm at a pace that set his feet on fire and burned them to stumps. Then the evil spirit had dropped him back to earth with a vicious hunger for human flesh. A hunger that still raged within.

He was still babbling when they tied him to a stake and burned him. The chief's wife lit the fire with steady hands and watched with hatred and satisfaction as the man who murdered her daughter burned.

Sickened, Snow Bird turned away, unable to watch the terrible creature Two Trees had become. It was over with his death. Of course it was. But around her, the temperature was dropping fast, and storm clouds were massing in the sky, and the howl of the wind was the howl of an evil spirit, its feast thwarted. In her nostrils, she smelled the stench of rotting fruit and animal musk, growing stronger as the blizzard approached.

That night, as the blizzard winds moaned and shrieked their deadly messages around the lodge, Snow Bird dreamed of summer. She was walking along her favorite stream, admiring the beauty around her, when suddenly the stream turned to ice, the ground around her frosted over, and a black mist as dark as a night devoid of stars rose in a cloud before her, taking on a vaguely human shape. The dark thing sucked on the eyes, pulling all light into its depths and utterly abolishing it. Red eyes gleamed from the place its head might have been—if it had a head—and a rotting tongue appeared in a hole that was totally unlike a mouth. "Sssnow Bird," the Wendigo hissed.

Deep inside the shadow, Snow Bird saw something pulsing with a bitter cold so deep that it burned her skin to be near it. It was the Wendigo's heart of ice. She stood frozen to the spot, unable to scream, unable to run, staring in heart-numbing terror at the dark cannibal spirit that had taken Two Trees.

Suddenly, a warm breeze swirled around her, and a bird landed upon her shoulder. Its tiny claws prickled through her shirt as it walked excitedly up and down her arm, its eyes fixed on the black cloud that was the cold spirit of the Wendigo. Then the spirit-bird spoke: "One thing kills Wendigo, Snow Bird. The knife of fire. When it comes, you must plunge the knife of fire into its frozen heart, or it will destroy you and everyone that you love. Remember." Then the little bird launched itself from her shoulder, screaming with rage. As it flew forward, it transformed into a stone knife with flames licking all along the blade. The knife drove itself right through the pulsing heart of ice within the Wendigo and out the other side. The Wendigo screamed, a sound so terrifying that Snow Bird screamed herself. It exploded upward in a cloud of ice and steam and dark flame, and the stone knife flew back toward Snow Bird and dropped gently into her hand.

A heartbeat later, she woke in Bearclaw's arms, trembling and sobbing while her poor frightened husband soothed her as best he could. It was only as they lay back down to sleep that Snow Bird realized that some kind of leather holder—that hadn't been there when she fell asleep—was now strapped around her thigh. Inside it was a long, narrow, pointed shape. She touched it gingerly, felt along its smoothly carved handle, its cold blade. It was the stone knife she had seen in her vision.

The blizzard raged on and on, hammering at the isolated village in a fury. The snow was so fierce and swirled so strongly in the blizzard winds that all sight was obscured. Snow Bird could not even make out the lodge of their neighbors, only yards away from their door. Not a glimmer of light showed through the swirling, howling snow. She and Bearclaw were alone in the storm. The cold crept closer and still closer. They huddled over the fire, drinking hot broth and staying warm as best they could. They were both uneasy in the dim twilight. Snow Bird's nostrils twitched every so often, as a sickly sweet stench of rotting fruit and animal musk wafted through the cracks of the lodge. The sense of menace approaching, of something huge and deadly ready to pounce silenced them. They clung together shamelessly as the day and night wore on. And finally they fell asleep, exhausted by fear, as the sounds of the storm grew dim and then ceased.

And then, through the empty silence that made the ears buzz after the howl of the storm, something spoke. "Bearclaw," it hissed. "Bearclaw." It was a summons.

The stench of rotting fruit and animal musk filled the lodge. Snow Bird's eyes popped open at once when she heard the voice. Bearclaw was already on his feet, his eyes wide-opened and hypnotized by the unearthly voice that called his name. He was quick, but Snow Bird was quicker. She flung herself out through the door of the lodge and ran—fast as an arrow—toward the towering darkness with the flaming red eyes and rotting tongue. Her hand was already gripping the knife as she screamed: "You will not have my husband!"

Bearclaw was right behind her, running forward in answer to the summons. He was fast and strong and would outpace her in a moment. There was only one thing to do, and Snow Bird did it. She drew back her arm and threw the knife straight at the pulsing light at the center of the evil spirit of the Wendigo. The knife turned over and over, and time slowed so that she saw every rotation of the blade as it flew through the air, even faster than Bearclaw could run. She was not particularly skilled in knife throwing, but this time, the spirits were with her. The knife burst into flame as it approached the dark spirit of the Wendigo, and the creature moved a moment too late as the flaming knife given to Snow Bird by the spirits lodged within its icy heart.

At once the Wendigo screamed, a terrible howl that woke the whole village. Flames licked the edges of the black spirit-flesh, and it suddenly exploded upward into a tower of searing

SNOW BIRD

brightness that knocked Bearclaw and Snow Bird off their feet. The Wendigo gave a keening wail of distress, and within its cry were the voices of its victims—Sings Like A Bird, Two Trees, Smiling Cloud, and many others.

Men, women, and children stumbled sleepily from their lodges and stood thigh-deep in snow, staring upward at the burning blackness that was the Wendigo. It shined for a long moment like a blazing star, swirling with light and darkness, and the stench of rot grew so strong it made many retch in revulsion. But the warm flames burned the smell away, and as it faded, so did the black spirit that was the Wendigo.

Snow Bird crawled through the icy drifts to her husband's stunned form. She hugged him tightly to her chest, ignoring the creeping cold behind and the blazing warmth before them. The cold was a good cold—the natural cold of winter. And the warmth came from the spirits who had sent her the knife of fire that could cut through a heart made of ice. Bearclaw stirred, opened his eyes, and gazed in awe at the burning fire that swirled in the treetops above him. "What happened?" he asked his wife, realizing that he was lying in a snowdrift in the darkness just before dawn.

"I killed the Wendigo," Snow Bird said, her voice trembling a little and her heart beating fast with joy. "It called you by name, and I killed it before it could take you."

Bearclaw's eyes widened as he took in this information. He stared, stricken, at the evil spirit that had wanted to do to him what it had done to Two Trees. Then he stared back at his very special, very gifted wife, and did not know what to say.

At that moment, the medicine man and the chief came quietly over to the young couple and helped them to their feet.

The medicine man took Snow Bird's hand in his and looked deeply into her eyes. "Thank you," he said. Snow Bird nodded her acknowledgement, unable to speak for the tears in her eyes.

Then, as the last of the unearthly fire faded from the treetops, the people let out a shout of joy, roaring out their relief and gratitude at the demise of the evil Wendigo. And the chief and his wife wept for their lost child and clung to each other in relief, knowing that their other children were no longer in danger. Snow Bird and Bearclaw stood close together and smiled and smiled as if they would never stop.

All her long life, Snow Bird was honored as a hero by her tribe, for it was she who had saved her people from the dark shadow that had overtaken them. And to this day, it is considered good luck to have a girl-child with wavy dark hair and eyes of an unusual golden-brown color with glints of green in their depths. When such a child is born, she is always named Snow Bird.

Resources

Asfar, Daniel. *Ghost Stories of America*. Edmonton, AB: Ghost House Books, 2001.

———. *Ghost Stories of Montana*. Auburn, WA: Lone Pine Publishing International, 2007.

Bakeless, John, ed. *The Journals of Lewis and Clark*. New York: Signet Classics, 2002.

Battle, Kemp P. *Great American Folklore*. New York: Doubleday & Company, Inc., 1986.

Baumler, Ellen. *Beyond Spirit Tailings*. Helena, MT: Montana Historical Society Press, 2005.

———. *Spirit Tailings*. Helena, MT: Montana Historical Society Press, 2002.

Botkin, B. A., ed. *A Treasury of American Folklore*. New York: Crown, 1944.

Brewer, J. Mason. *American Negro Folklore*. Chicago: Quadrangle Books, 1972.

Brown, D. *Legends*. Eugene, OR: Randall V. Mills Archive of Northwest Folklore at the University of Oregon, 1971.

Brunvand, Jan Harold. *The Choking Doberman and Other Urban Legends*. New York: W. W. Norton, 1984.

———. *The Vanishing Hitchhiker*. New York: W. W. Norton, 1981.

Coffin, Tristram. P., and Hennig Cohen, eds. *Folklore in America*. New York: Doubleday & AMP, 1966.

———. *Folklore from the Working Folk of America*. New York: Doubleday, 1973.

Cohen, Daniel, and Susan Cohen. *Hauntings & Horrors*. New York: Dutton Children's Books, 2002.

Cornplanter, J. J. *Legends of the Longhouse*. Philadelphia: J. B. Lippincott, 1938.

Dorson, R. M. *America in Legend*. New York: Pantheon Books, 1973.

Downer, Deborah L. *Classic American Ghost Stories*. Little Rock, AR: August House Publishers, Inc., 1990.

Editors of Life. *The Life Treasury of American Folklore*. New York: Time Inc., 1961.

Enss, Chris. *Tales Behind the Tombstones*. Helena, MT: Globe Pequot, 2007.

Erdoes, Richard, and Alfonso Ortiz. *American Indian Myths and Legends*. New York: Pantheon Books, 1984.

Fifer, Barbara. *Montana Mining Ghost Towns*. Helena, MT: Farcountry Press, 2002.

Flanagan, J. T., and A. P. Hudson. *The American Folk Reader*. New York: A. S. Barnes & Co., 1958.

Fugleber, Paul. *Montana Nessie of Flathead Lake*. Polson, MT: Treasure State Publishing Co., Inc., 1992.

Grande, Irene Ford, and the Metis Cultural Recovery Oral History Collection. *Irene Ford Grande Interview*. Helena, MT: Montana Historical Society Archives, 1994.

Larios, Shellie. Yellowstone Ghost Stories. Helena, MT: Riverbend Publishing, 2006.

Leach, M. *The Rainbow Book of American Folk Tales and Legends*. New York: The World Publishing Co., 1958.

Leeming, David, and Jake Pagey. *Myths, Legends, & Folktales of America*. New York: Oxford University Press, 1999.

Montana Folklife Project. *Montana Folklife Project Records, 1979–1992, Box 3, Folders 14–18: When the Work's All Done This Fall*. Helena, MT: Montana Historical Society Archives, 1980.

Montana Folklife Project, and Jill Ronan. *Montana Folklife Project Records, 1979–1992, Box 1, Folder 17: Our Own Calamity Jane: Field Research Paper*. Helena, MT: Montana Historical Society Archives, 1981.

Mott, A. S. *Ghost Stories of America, Vol. II*. Edmonton, AB: Ghost House Books, 2003.

Munn, Debra D. *Big Sky Ghosts, Volume One*. Boulder, CO: Pruett Publishing Company, 1993.

———. *Big Sky Ghosts, Volume Two*. Boulder, CO: Pruett Publishing Company, 1994.

———. *Montana Ghost Stories*. Helena, MT: Riverbend Publishing, 2007.

Murray, Earl. *Ghosts of the Old West*. Chicago: Contemporary Books, 1988.

No Runner, Vernon. *Sta-ai-tsi-nix-sin: Ghost stories.* Browning, MT: Blackfeet Heritage Program, 1954.

Norman, Michael, and Beth Scott. *Historic Haunted America.* New York: Tor Books, 1995.

Peck, Catherine, ed. *A Treasury of North American Folk Tales.* New York: W. W. Norton, 1998.

Polley, J., ed. *American Folklore and Legend.* New York: Reader's Digest Association, 1978.

Reevy, Tony. *Ghost Train!* Lynchburg, VA: TLC Publishing, 1998.

Rogers, Ms., and English III Section A Class. *Encounters of the Supernatural.* Wilbaux, MT: Montana Historical Society Research Center Archives, 2002.

Rule, Leslie. *Coast to Coast Ghosts.* Kansas City, KS: Andrews McMeel Publishing, 2001.

Schwartz, Alvin. *Scary Stories to Tell in the Dark.* New York: Harper Collins, 1981.

Skinner, Charles M. *American Myths and Legends,* Vol. 1. Philadelphia: J. B. Lippincott, 1903.

———. *Myths and Legends of Our Own Land,* Vols. 1 & 2. Philadelphia: J. B. Lippincott, 1896.

Spence, Lewis. *North American Indians: Myths and Legends Series.* London: Bracken Books, 1985.

Stevens, Karen. *Haunted Montana.* Helena, MT: Riverbend Publishing, 2007.

Walter, Dave. *Montana Campfire Tales.* Helena, MT: TwoDot, 1997.

Whealdon, Bon I, and others. *I Will Be Meat for My Salish.* Helena, MT: Montana Historical Society Press, 2001.

White, D. *Folk Narratives.* Eugene, OR: Randall V. Mills Archive of Northwest Folklore at the University of Oregon, 1971.

Zeitlin, Steven J., Amy J. Kotkin, and Holly Cutting Baker. *A Celebration of American Family Folklore.* New York: Pantheon Books, 1982.

About the Author

S. E. Schlosser has been telling stories since she was a child, when games of "let's pretend" quickly built themselves into full-length tales acted out with friends. A graduate of Houghton College, the Institute of Children's Literature, and Rutgers University, she created and maintains the award-winning Web site Americanfolklore.net, where she shares a wealth of stories from all fifty states, some dating back to the origins of America. She spends much of her time answering questions from visitors to the site. Many of her favorite e-mails come from other folklorists who delight in practicing the old tradition of "who can tell the tallest tale."

About the Illustrator

Artist Paul Hoffman trained in painting and printmaking, with his first extensive illustration work on assignment in Egypt, drawing ancient wall reliefs for the University of Chicago. His work graces books of many genres—children's titles, textbooks, short story collections, natural history volumes, and numerous cookbooks. For *Spooky Montana,* he employed a scratchboard technique and an active imagination.